SONGS
from
HOME

Nov 19, 1994

*For Livvie Ste &
Julie,

Dear Friends —
Have a good read —

Love,
[signature]*

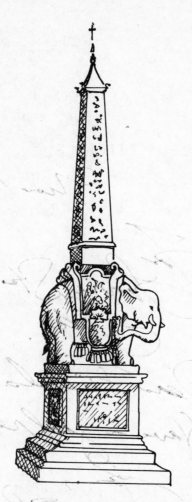

Elephant by Bernini
Piazza della Minerva

JOAN ELIZABETH GOODMAN

SONGS
from
HOME

Illustrations by the author

HARCOURT BRACE & COMPANY
San Diego New York London

"Bye Bye Blackbird"
Lyric by Mort Dixon; music by Ray Henderson. Copyright © 1926. Copyright renewed 1953. All rights for the extended term of copyright administered by Fred Ahlert Music Corporation on behalf of Olde Clover Leaf Music. Ray Henderson share administered by Ray Henderson Music. Used by permission. All rights reserved.

Library of Congress Cataloging-in-Publication Data
Goodman, Joan E.
    Songs from home/Joan Elizabeth Goodman.—1st ed.
        p.   cm.
    Summary: In Rome in 1969, after years of being adrift in Europe, eleven-year-old Anna and her father sing in the streets for money, while Anna dreams of having a normal home and family life.
    ISBN 0-15-203590-7 ISBN 0-15-203591-5 (pbk.)
    [1. Rome (Italy)—Fiction.   2. Street music and musicians—Fiction.   3. Fathers and daughters—Fiction.]   I. Title.
PZ7.G61375So   1994
[Fic]—dc20   93-46248

The text type was set in Garamond #3.

Designed by Kaelin Chappell

Printed in Hong Kong

First edition

A B C D E

This book is dedicated to the memory of my father and to my husband, Keith, the devoted father of Juliet Eve.

I also gratefully acknowledge the encouragement and astute editorial guidance of Margaret Gabel and her writing workshop.

CONTENTS

PREFACE

Street performers threaded their way from restaurant to restaurant through the center of Rome, singing and begging for tips. Out of the velvet night came a man with a young girl. The man carried a battered guitar. The girl wore a dress too thin for the damp autumn air. They both looked ragged and worn.

They were Americans, and this was their song:

Blackbird, blackbird singing the blues
    all day,
right outside of my door.
Blackbird, blackbird, gotta be on my way,
where there's sunshine galore.

Pack up all my care and woe,
here I go singing low,
bye bye blackbird. . . .

PENSIONE AURIGA

Anna was having a hard time at the Pensione
Auriga. Concentrating on her math homework
was only part of it. The *pensione* was a cross
between a run-down boardinghouse and the
cheapest of hotels. It was where people who
could leave left quickly and those who didn't
have a choice stayed.

The remains of *pranzo,* the midday dinner,
had been cleared away. All the boarders, except
for the German students, had gone to their
rooms for *siesta.* Anna sat leaning over the table
in the murky dining room. Both her hands
held back her unruly thatch of blond hair as
she stared at a sea of fractions. She hated these
splintered numbers. Dividing fractions, mul-
tiplying them—it always amounted to the
same thing: more prickly, broken numbers.

"*Quel Americano,* Hop-a-kinza! *Lui e pigro!
Pigro, pigro, PIGRO!*"

That was Signora Rossi in the kitchen, complaining again about Papa, Stephen *Hopkins*. Not *Hop-a-kinza!* And he was *not* lazy. The "Signora" was an old hag who hated all of her boarders, especially Anna and Papa, probably because they were Americans. What drove Anna crazy was that Papa hardly seemed to notice her or anything else about this awful place.

The room was stifling and thick with the smoke from Signor Rossi's endless cigarettes. Every day was the same. Anna struggled with her homework, feeling groggy and sick from the smoke and the Signora's famous "heavy spaghetti" made with potatoes, oil, and garlic. She had tried doing her homework upstairs in their room, but that was worse. Papa snored and thrashed about, and there wasn't a table to work on. She wanted to be in the warm, clean kitchen, but the Signora had said she got in the way of Maria's work. Maria was Anna's special friend and a wonderful cook. *She'd* never serve heavy spaghetti. But the Signora wouldn't let Maria cook for the *pensione,* only for the Rossis. She made Maria do all the cleaning, laundry, and dishes, and she kept Maria running errands from morning to night.

"Stupida! Cretina!" shouted the Signora. "I will send you back to starve in Calabria!"

Then Anna heard a loud slap. How could Maria stand working for that witch? Maria said it was only until she turned twenty. Then she would be able to go home with enough money to marry Tonio.

"Two years is not such a long time to wait for freedom *and* Tonio."

Anna wished she had a home waiting for her, a place where she truly belonged. America might be that place. At least in America no one would tease her about being an American. If only Papa would take them back.

At last the Signora stopped shouting, but Anna still couldn't concentrate on dividing $5/16$ into $6/8$. Signor Rossi was hunched over his crossword puzzle, an inch-long cigarette ash hovering above the page. One after another he snipped the cheap black cigarettes in half, fitted them in his holder, and lit up. How could he sit there for hours barely moving, barely alive, and yet still manage to flick the ash into the silver dish at just the right moment? What if one day the ash missed the silver dish and, as in a happy-ending fairy tale, Signor Rossi woke up? Anna could see it all clearly in her mind. First he would silence the Signora and double Maria's salary. Then he'd open the shutters and the windows. Fresh air and sunshine would invade the room. Papa would walk in, dazzled by the sunlight and sweet breeze. Finally, he too would awaken and realize that they didn't belong in Rome. And he would take Anna home.

Signor Rossi gently tapped his cigarette. The ash dropped silently into the silver dish.

Anna and her father had been adrift in Europe for almost as long as she could remember. She was nearly twelve now, and she thought they'd left America when she was between two and three. But Papa wouldn't talk about this. He'd make a dumb joke or simply change the subject if she asked about it. Sometimes he'd talk a little bit about when he was growing up in Missouri. There was fishing for bass at dawn in a nearby pond and family dinners of chicken-fried steak with biscuits and gravy. It sounded great to Anna—growing up in a big family, living out in the country. But Papa ended every story saying "Thank God I made it to Europe, to a place where you and I can live freely."

Something bad had happened there. Maybe it was something about her mother. Whatever it was, it made Papa sad and edgy if she started asking too many questions. If she pressed him too much, his eyes would go blank and his face would close up tight. He'd say "That's enough!" and nothing more. And then she was left so terribly alone. It was better not to pester him. Someday she'd find out what had happened. But she wouldn't make Papa tell her, not if it hurt him that much.

They'd stayed in Rome longer than anywhere else. Maybe this was a good sign. It could mean that Papa was finally settling down. But settling down in a third-rate boarding-house tucked in a back alley by the Pantheon was not what Anna had in mind when she thought of home. Home had always meant being with Papa, but lately that wasn't enough. She wanted more—a real home in a place where she belonged.

Signor Rossi took out a new cigarette, snipped it in half, put one half into the ebony holder, and went back to his crossword puzzle.

Papa came into the room, his straw-colored hair a wild halo, still dazed from his nap. He was thin and young looking, except for his eyes. Anna looked up into those cloudy gray eyes, the exact shade of her own, and asked, "Can I go with you?"

"Go where? What?"

"You know, you always go for an espresso."

"Yes, I do."

"So?"

"Okay, yeah . . . sure . . . come along."

"I'll get my jacket."

She grabbed her homework, raced with it up three flights to their room, and was back down the stairs, wearing her maroon school jacket, so fast that Papa was still rooted to the spot where she'd left him. Signor Rossi looked up as they headed for the door. Was he seeing them off or merely searching the air for a five-letter word?

Via dei Cornacchie was only just beginning to waken from its midday doze. Most of the shops were still shuttered and blank looking, the jumbled shapes and colors of their window displays hidden behind the roll-down metal doors. Anna liked this quiet Rome best. It wasn't so busy showing off and making noise. It was like an ancient grandmother who had seen and done everything and now sat quietly in the shade. The city smelled of the ages past, especially as they walked by cellar gratings where the air was cool and moldy.

Papa was singing softly. Even in the quiet street, Anna could barely catch his words. But the melody came out sweet and true, a little silver stream of music in the drowsy street. Three artisans who repaired fancy old furniture looked up from their sanding and smiled. They were much better than Papa's usual audience of smug *signori* forking in their pasta.

It was such a waste. Papa shouldn't have been a singing beggar for rude pigs. And neither should she.

She could only stand the begging because singing with Papa was so beautiful *and* so far no one from school had caught her doing it. Everything went smoothly at school as long as you were part of the group, keeping in step with everyone else. Being "The American" was bad enough. If anyone found out about the street singing, it would turn her into one of the class lepers. Then she might as well crawl into some corner and die. She found this out at her first school in Rome. The kids gave her such a hard time, she made Papa go to the Ministry of Public Education and pretend that they were moving to the suburbs. She enrolled at La Madama, way out by the old Olympic stadium, nearly an hour's ride by bus each morning. But the long ride was worth it. The kids who went to La Madama had hardly ever been to the old Roman center, and they'd never go there at night. Anna's secrets were safe.

Anna and Papa came to Corso Rinascimento, one of the main streets of Rome, where horns squealed and engines roared as the Romans battled their way back to work after the midday break. Across the *corso* they followed a narrow street that led to the piazza.

She could never get used to the blare of Roman traffic. And in a different way, she could never get used to the beauty of Piazza Navona. It was always a surprise—a wonderful surprise—to come from the dark, winding streets to the wide open space of the elegant square. This was where all good things were possible. It was the exact opposite of Pensione Auriga.

Anna led the way into the café and up to the cashier's perch.

"We would like one long *caffè* and one cappuccino, please," she said.

Papa dug into his pocket and came up with a crumpled bill and some change that spilled out of his hand, jangling all over the marble floor. She cringed. It wasn't such a big deal; people dropped money all the time. She shouldn't let it bother her. But Anna always tried to slip by unnoticed and Papa always did something that stood out. Anna scrambled around helping her father retrieve the coins. Finally, he paid the cashier. Anna took the receipt over to the bar, where they stood alongside the other customers. It cost five hundred lira extra to sit at the tables under the portico or on the piazza. So every day they stood at the bar.

"Tell me," said the barman.

"One long *caffé*," said Anna, "and one cappuccino."

The bar was almost too sleek—all shiny stainless steel and glass. Sometimes it gave her chills. But she loved watching the barman wring *caffés* out of the giant espresso machine, and the smells of black coffee, steamed milk with cinnamon, and the pastries.

The barman plunked down their two cups. Anna spooned sugar into her cup, sinking the foam on top of her cappuccino. Then she nudged Papa. He looked at her blankly.

"Tip," she whispered, pointing with her chin at the little dish next to the sugar bowl.

Papa put a hundred-lira coin in the dish.

"That's too much!" said Anna.

"Don't worry about all these little things, Anna-Banana. It'll wrinkle you."

"Anna," she said. "No Banana, no Tutta-Panna, no Fandana—just Anna."

"Yes'm," said Papa, smiling. "I'll try to remember."

Not that he would. He was always fancying up her name. He had added the extra *a* in the first place. She wished he'd kept it as her mother had wanted. Because that's what Anna wanted, to be simply Ann Hopkins.

She cradled the cup of cappuccino in both hands and went over to the pastry counter. What would it be like to eat each and every creamy, luscious one? One hundred lira would buy one third of that *cannole*. Anna laughed out loud. How *could* she have been thinking about fractions!

Papa put down his cup and ambled out of the café. Anna took one last gulp and followed after him.

They were weaving through the tables when she noticed a jacket exactly like her own. She tried to duck behind a column, but it was too late. Fiorella, her friend from school, had already spotted her.

"*Ciao,* Anna!" Fiorella bounded out of her seat, rushing over to her like an enthusiastic puppy. She touched Anna's sleeve, her hand, her hair.

"How are you? What are you doing here?

You're not alone? Come and sit with us. Meet my parents. Come, Anna, come!"

"I can't stay," said Anna. "I'm with my father."

"Good! He can sit with us, too!"

"Oh, no!" said Anna. "I mean, he can't. . . . He . . ."

"Well, then you come," said Fiorella, and she guided Anna to their table.

The Mazzinis seemed much older than Papa and more settled looking, but then, most parents were.

"Ah, so you are the American girl." Signor Mazzini extended his hand and smiled warmly.

"It's a pleasure to meet you," said Signora Mazzini. She held Anna's hand with both of hers. "Fiorella tells me all about you."

Anna felt a moment of panic. What had Fiorella told her? But Signora Mazzini kept smiling brightly. She should stop being so tense. Signora Mazzini was just being kind.

"It's nice to meet you," said Anna. "But my father has gone on ahead. I'd better catch up with him. Please excuse me."

"I'll walk with you a ways," said Fiorella. "May I, Babo?"

"Five minutes," said Signor Mazzini. "I

mean it, Fiorella. We have to pick up your brothers and start unpacking."

Fiorella hooked onto Anna's arm and they started across the square.

"What are you doing here?" asked Anna. "Shopping?"

"No, we just moved into a new apartment right nearby."

Anna froze. "You didn't tell me you were moving here!"

"Well"—Fiorella looked uncomfortable—"I didn't tell anyone. You live near here, too, don't you?"

"Well, sort of, not really."

"My father will let me keep on at La Madama so I can be with my friends."

"Um," said Anna.

"I told him that if you could ride the bus in from the center, so could I."

"Why didn't you tell me you were moving?" Anna couldn't believe this was happening.

Fiorella shook her head, flinging back her chestnut hair like she was shaking off the question.

"It happened very quickly. But isn't it good, Anna? Now we can see each other every day after school, even at night. We can ride the bus together tomorrow morning. Won't it be great?"

The heavy spaghetti turned a somersault in Anna's stomach. "Sure," she said. "It will be great."

HISTORY LESSON

Anna caught up with her father at the far side of Piazza Navona. He was sitting on the steps in front of the church of Sant'Agnese, staring at the central fountain. She sat down next to him.

"So what do you think, Anna-Banana?" he asked.

He was hopeless. And so was her future at La Madama. Living right around the corner, Fiorella was bound to find out that she lived in a cruddy *pensione* and sang for tips in restaurants. Maybe she should start looking for a school in E.U.R., the suburbs on the other side of Rome, which was even farther away from the center.

"Hey, Anna! What's doing? You okay?"

She looked hard at Papa. What could she tell him? She didn't want to worry him or hurt his feelings. He seemed so fragile, almost like a child. If only he were older and more ordinary, more like Signor Mazzini, more like a father. She sighed and leaned against his shoulder. He put his arm around her, and they sat quietly like that for a few peaceful minutes.

"That is the Fountain of the Four Rivers. Each one of those figures represents a great river."

Papa was speaking softly, almost crooning. The October sun was warm on her knees. There was plenty of time to worry later. She settled in to listen to Papa's story.

"There's the Danube, Ganges, and Nile," said Papa, pointing out the figures. "That one with his arm raised up like the church is going to fall on his head is the Rio de la Plata."

Anna nodded.

"The story goes that Bernini, who designed the fountain, hated Borromini, the architect of Sant'Agnese." Papa gestured to the church behind them. "The fountain was his way of saying that the church was ugly and Borromini was a jerk."

It was like the jokes that got passed around the classroom about "Fat Luigi." Fiorella called those mean little jokes *cattiverie* and laughed. A *cattiveria* carved in stone with all of Rome laughing seemed more than naughty—it was evil.

"But it isn't true," said Papa.

"What isn't true?"

"The fountain was finished way before the church was even begun."

"So what does the statue mean?"

Papa shrugged.

"Mother used to say—"

"My grandmother?"

"Yes, Banana, your grandmother used to say that people were more interested in the feuding and misery of others than the truth of the matter. She had reason to know that only too well."

"Why?" This was the story she really wanted to hear.

"Your grandmother held onto the truth and her own dignity when the whole town was abuzz with malicious gossip. Now, can I get on with my story?"

Anna was silent. She'd rather hear more about her grandmother than about two dead Italians.

"The point is that the feud between Bernini and Borromini is the story that's lasted because it's more interesting."

"But if it's a lie—"

"It's a lie that's lasted for three hundred years."

"It's not fair," said Anna.

Fountain of the Four Rivers
Piazza Navona

"Nothing much is fair," said Papa. "Have you finished your homework?"

"Speaking of unfair!"

"Well?"

"No," she said. "I'm stuck on the fractions."

"Come on," said Papa. "I'll give you a hand." He stood up and held out his hand. Anna took it, smiling in spite of herself. His jokes were always so stupid and his stories so confusing.

They headed out of the piazza, along the awakening streets, back to Pensione Auriga.

"I still don't get it," she said.

"Don't get what?"

Papa had drifted into one of his clouds. Did he even remember what they were talking about?

"I don't get the story about the fountain and the church."

"People will think whatever they want to think. The truth rarely matters. That is the story."

Had some of his truths been twisted into lies? How did that fit in with her grandmother's story, or her own?

Anna had touched up her own story to make it seem more normal. For starters, she lied about her age. But she was so small, no one guessed how much older she was than the other kids in her class. She told them Papa had a job with the F.A.O., the Food and Agricultural Organization, which had something to do with the United Nations. She'd also invented a nice apartment for them near the Pantheon. She said Papa sent her to school at La Madama so she could get some fresh air every day. Gina and Teresa, two girls from school, thought it was nuts, but the need for fresh air fit in with her being an American.

Her invented stories made much more sense than her real life, which was so puzzling. The biggest puzzle was Anna's mother. Papa told plenty of fairy tales about her. In Anna's favorite story her mother was a magic swan who became human just long enough to marry Papa and give birth to Anna. Then she flew back to her golden castle on the sapphire lake. Every so often, Papa said, she flew by to make sure Anna was doing all right. They'd often see swans at a city park or on a country pond. And there was always one swan that seemed to look at Anna in a special, caring way.

Only once, long ago, Papa had told her that her mother had died and gone to Heaven. It made him so sad to tell her, it seemed like days before he really smiled again. Whenever she tried to find out more about her mother and how she died, Papa would get so sad he'd sort of fold in on himself. So she listened carefully to all his fairy tales, hoping that real clues about her mother were buried in the stories. If she was very clever, she might be able to figure it all out on her own.

Anna looked up. They were back on Via dei Cornacchie.

Pensione Auriga was oddly quiet as they entered the murky hallway where the Signora stashed mildewed trunks with broken locks, several wobbly tables, and chairs whose stuffing had burst through their faded covers.

"Well, well," said Papa. "The Salvation Army still hasn't picked up."

That was another joke, not that Anna ever got it. Papa said it nearly every time they walked in the door. "You had to be there," he said, "there" meaning America.

The dining room was empty, but Signor Rossi's cloud of cigarette smoke remained, fouling the room.

"Let's do my homework upstairs," said Anna.

"Let's *you* do your homework upstairs."

"You said you'd help me."

"I will."

They started up the long, dark stairs. The Signora must have been out. The house was never this quiet with her around. The German students were either out or asleep. They were loud, too, stomping around in hiking boots, shaking the whole house. The *vecchiette,* the old ladies, were probably tucked safely in their rooms. Anna shuddered as they passed by all the closed doors. There were a handful of *vecchiette* who lived at the *pensione,* quiet as mice. They acted like mice, too, skittering along the hallways to and from the bathroom or the *gabinetto,* a stinking, ancient toilet with yesterday's newspaper cut up for wipes. The old women were so frightened of everything, they gave Anna the willies.

When they reached the third-floor landing, Anna sniffed, then pinched her nose.

"He's back," she whispered.

Signor Tomaso shuttled between his room in the *pensione* and a farmhouse out near Ostia. There was no mistaking his return. The whole third floor reeked of his cheap black cigars and old, never-washed self. His door opened, and he came shuffling out in his slippers to greet them.

"Caught again!" said Papa under his breath, giving Signor Tomaso a weak smile.

Signor Tomaso backed them into the far corner of the hall and started wheezing and garbling in a Neapolitan dialect that neither Anna nor Papa could begin to understand. He wore a grease-stained, food-encrusted plaid robe. Anna moved behind Papa to get as far from him and the smell as possible.

"*Si, si,*" said Papa. "Certainly you must be right." He gently edged her to their door, nodding his head, looking serious, agreeing. Signor Tomaso was turning quite red. He stabbed the air with his cigar, talking louder and louder.

Papa unlocked the door.

"Good day," he said and pulled Anna into their room.

Once inside, he slumped against the door, rolling his eyes, and Anna collapsed on her bed, laughing. Signor Tomaso seemed funny, but only when Papa was with her.

Anna looked up at the lumpy, cracked ceiling, her own private gallery. If she squinted her eyes just so, she saw a tiger with a crooked tail or a one-eyed man with a beard. Her bed was over by the window. Papa's was in the opposite corner of the small room, facing the battered armoire.

"That's fine with me," he had said. "*I* don't need a view."

Her "view" was a blank stucco wall. Still, she liked the fresh air and looking up at the sky, watching clouds and the swallows swooping overhead.

Down at a window on the second floor, one of the *vecchiette* sat leaning on her sill, looking out all day long. What did she see? Not much went on in the courtyard. Maria hung out the laundry, cats napped in the sun, occasionally Signora Rossi appeared, complaining. Perhaps there was another old woman at the opposite window and all day long they watched each other.

Anna got out her homework and flopped back down on her bed. Papa sat with her, and before long he'd untangled the worst of the fractions. She slogged through the rest of the math on her own. Occasionally she looked up at Papa, who sat propped up against his pillows, his guitar resting like a giant platter across his knees. He stroked the strings very gently, humming to himself, dreaming his dreams. He was so content with the way things were, with the roaming, even the begging. He talked about being free, telling Anna how lucky they were, how like the birds. But even birds had their own nests. Papa didn't seem aware of that.

Once the math was finished, she whipped through the geography homework and then started her reading assignment. It was what she liked best, and she saved it for last, like dessert.

"Anna-Banana, you should start getting ready. It's almost time to go."

She looked out the window. The stucco glowed a deep copper color in the setting sun. She put down her book. How could it already be evening?

"Okay," she said. "I'll go change."

Anna had special clothes she wore to work. They were old clothes, meant to look old. The dress she wore was once blue with yellow flowers. Now it had gone to pale gray and the flowers were brownish splotches. The sleeves ended too soon and the hem barely reached her knees. She wore a faded sweater that had started out with six buttons but now had only two. She wanted to look as different as possible from the girl who was in the fifth elementary at La Madama. When she first started singing with Papa she put on her prettiest clothes as if she were giving a concert. When she got older,

she saw how silly that was. They weren't singers on a stage, they were beggars in the street.
Anna began to hate those pretty dresses. That's
when she decided to wear something different,
a sort of beggar costume. The trouble was, once
she put it on, she felt like a beggar, too.

Anna changed in the bathroom, avoiding her
image in the big oval mirror above the sink.
Back in their room, she hung her day clothes
in the armoire, giving her school jacket little
pats, smoothing it out, before she shut the
armoire's doors.

"I'll go down to the kitchen now."

"Meet you outside," said Papa.

Anna nodded, left the room, and hurried
down the stairs as quietly as possible.

This was the first awful part of their evening
ritual. Anna snuck down to the kitchen where
Maria had prepared them a snack. Only a continental breakfast and *pranzo* were included in
their rates. The evening meal would have been
extra, too much extra. Besides, they didn't
have time to sit and eat. When Maria found
out they were skipping supper, she came to
Papa with this plan. How she managed was
beyond Anna, as the Signora kept an eagle eye
on every lira and crumb. Even so, each evening
Maria had something ready for them. She gave

Anna a package wrapped in paper and a quick hug.

"Tonight will be lucky for you, Piccolina."

"But Mondays are never good nights for tips," whispered Anna.

"Tonight will be different," said Maria. "Trust me."

Anna smiled, hid the package in her schoolbag, and slipped out of the kitchen.

She hated to think what would happen if they ever got caught. She and Papa would be kicked out. But as for Maria, what would the Signora do to her?

Maria's snack was the best meal of the day. Even a plain omelet tasted better than anything the Signora served. But every time Anna left the kitchen, carrying the stolen food, her heart pounding, jumping at every little noise, she wondered if it was worth it. Tonight there was a new worry: whether or not Fiorella and her family were dining out.

III

SONGS FROM HOME

Papa was waiting for Anna in the little square at the end of Via dei Cornacchie. The square was called Largo Giuseppe Toniolo, such a big name for an extra bit of pavement and a slightly larger slice of sky. Anna approached carefully. Fiorella could be living right here in this tiny square. What if she came out and saw Anna in these clothes? What would she think? What could Anna say?

Papa was leaning against a doorway with his guitar slung over his shoulder. He looked so comfortable, he could have been asleep. Anna shivered; the sun was down and the shaded stone square was chilly. She pulled her sweater tighter, hugging her schoolbag, and went over to rouse Papa.

"Okay," she said. "Let's go."

His gray eyes unclouded. He looked at her, surprised and smiling.

"Anna-Fandana!" he said. "Yes, let's go."

They walked along one of the main streets heading for Trastevere. Anna glanced now and then over her shoulder, imagining Fiorella behind her, until Papa said, "Did you join the CIA or the Secret Service or something without telling me?"

And that made her stop. The traffic was at its worst. There was a constant clamor of horns and angry shouts as everyone, fed up with the fourth and last commute of the day, struggled to get home. Papa began walking faster and faster. Anna hurried along, trying to keep up. Why were they rushing along with the traffic as if *they* had somewhere important to go?

They crossed the river at Ponte Garibaldi, on the way to Piazza Santa Maria in Trastevere. They started the evening there at one of the tourists' restaurants. Tourists, especially Americans, usually tipped pretty well.

Anna and Papa came into the piazza right across from the church and in front of GianCarlo's Trattoria. Anna took a quick look around. There wasn't a Mazzini in sight.

"Ready?" asked Papa.

Anna stood so she could look at the golden mosaic on the church. It showed the Virgin Mary with some ladies carrying lamps. And it gave her enough courage to open her mouth and sing.

"Ready," she said.

Papa played a few chords and began.

Oh Shenandoah, I long to hear you,
Away, you rolling river. . . .

Papa never told her what they would sing. He just began and Anna joined in. They sang the songs Papa learned when he was growing up. He said the American tourists were all a little bit homesick and liked hearing something from the heartland of America, something from "those imaginary 'good ole days.'" Anna liked it, too. Singing those songs, she felt as if part of America belonged to her. It was the land of her heart, her dream of home.

"Besides," Papa had said, "these are the only songs I know."

He never made jokes to entertain the people. He didn't need to, his voice was enough. He stood quite still, strummed his guitar, and sang.

Away, I'm bound away,
Across the wide Missouri. . . .

His voice was deep and rolling like the river, washing over her, making everything seem all right. If the people weren't too busy eating or writing postcards, they felt it, too. He quieted them. Her own voice blended in higher and lighter. They were two ribbons of song weaving the melody. Anna stared at the glittering mosaic with dusk smudging the hard edges of stone and brick. She could almost make herself forget where they were and what they were doing.

Every night she studied the picture of Mary holding baby Jesus. Had her mother held her that tenderly? Someday she'd like a little baby of her own to hold. She'd had a doll once, named Charlotte. She was much too old now for dolls, but now and again she missed the cozy feeling of holding Charlotte.

The sky had turned a navy blue behind the church. The Angelus rang. Evening was well under way. Papa sang:

I've been working on the railroad,
All the livelong day. . . .

It was hard to picture him working on the railroad, especially the part about "rising up so early in the morning."

Mingled with their song were the clatter of crockery and the chattering diners. The smells of good food rose from the tables. Garlic was

the strongest scent, but there were other luscious smells, too—lamb roasted in rosemary,
baked clams with oregano, and the flowery
smell of fresh basil on blood-red tomato salads.
Her stomach growled. What had Maria tucked
into the brown paper parcel for their supper?

Papa had started singing "Down by the
Riverside."

Gonna lay down my sword and shield. . . .

They sang this song a lot the summer they
had lived on an apple farm in France, before
they came to Rome. Lots of people came to
live and work on the farm from all over Europe,
Canada, the United States, and even Japan.
Papa made friends with everyone. He spoke all
the different languages and even learned some
Japanese. They were three perfect months;
every single day seemed sunny. Anna ran
around all day with the other kids who traveled
Europe with their parents. They climbed the
apple trees and waded in a nearby stream. At
night everyone sat around a fire and sang songs.
And it wasn't one bit corny. It was almost like
having a real family, and Anna never wanted
any of it to end.

Then Peter showed up. He knew friends of
Papa's in Missouri. Anna hung around him all

the time, asking questions about America. Peter didn't know her mother, didn't even know her name. But he told Anna all about baseball games and hot dogs. He taught her the words to the Mickey Mouse Club song. It was best of all when he talked about Missouri. It sounded so pretty, especially in the summertime. Peter said Papa was famous in Willow Springs. He was known as a "cool dude with a monster Hog." That meant he had a big motorcycle. The more she talked to Peter, the more nervous Papa became. Then one day he packed their bags, and the next they were on the road to Rome. At the time, it didn't make any sense. Perhaps now she understood. Seeing someone from home made Papa feel the way she would if Fiorella saw her street singing. Anna would have changed schools. Papa had to go farther; he changed countries.

I ain't gonna study war no more.
I ain't gonna study war no more. . . .

The song was over. Now came the worst part. After three or four songs, Papa handed Anna his old French beret. She walked from table to table, holding out the hat and keeping her eyes on the littered cobblestones or studying the food on the tables. It was easier to pretend she wasn't there if she didn't look at the people. Besides, the food was more interesting. There were all kinds of pasta with red, green, and white sauces. Fish, chicken, and veal were grilled or stewed. Roasted peppers and steamed artichokes swam in pools of garlic and oil. She'd eat it all if she could.

She had snaked her way past most of the tables. The beret was partly filled with small change.

"Thank you," she said. "Thank you, thank you."

Papa insisted that she be polite, even if someone only gave a five-lira coin.

She approached the table of an older couple, who were Americans by the look of their clothes, cameras, and shopping bags. The woman clicked her tongue. Anna's skin prickled. She would *not* be pitied! She started to walk past the table.

"One second, dear," said the woman, catching hold of Anna's sleeve.

She turned to her husband, who had just stuffed his mouth with a forkful of rigatoni.

"Wha—?" he mumbled.

"Tip!" The woman spat out the word.

The man fished in his pocket and pulled out a ten-lira coin.

"Herbert, don't be a scrooge. Look at the child!"

"Excuse me," said Anna, trying to move away. But now the woman had a firm grip on her arm.

"Damn nuisance," said Herbert. He got out his wallet and handed Anna a thousand-lira bill. "Tell your father to get a job."

Fat pig! It was none of his business. She wanted to throw the money back in his face. But they needed it. She swallowed hard, her throat hot and tight.

"Thank you," she said to the woman, who finally released her.

"Hey! Stop bothering my customers. Off with you!" The restaurant manager suddenly appeared, shooing Anna away.

Bothering customers! She was glad to get away, to escape the Americans. She hurried back to Papa's side, so upset and shaky the coins were dancing in the beret.

"Annalina." Papa took the beret from her and squeezed her hand. "Don't be upset. It's no big deal getting thrown out. He's just looking for a kickback. You should know that."

Papa led her away from the restaurant to sit on the fountain steps. She couldn't look at him. If she did, she'd start crying.

Café Scene

"Did he say something mean?"

"No, not really," she said. "I'm just mad."

She was mad, so mad she could hardly breathe. Those stupid Americans. That greedy manager. And Papa. Papa! She couldn't be mad at Papa. There he was, stroking her hand, looking at her, so worried.

"I only got partway through the tables. We lost half our tips."

"It doesn't matter," he said.

"Of course it matters!"

They needed that money for the *pensione,* her bus fares and school stuff, and Papa's *caffés* and newspapers. That didn't even include things like clothes and books. Why was it *he* never worried about money?

"Well, simmer down, Banana. Let's see what goodies Maria packed for us tonight."

Papa unwrapped the neat parcel, while Anna clenched and unclenched her fists. He had no idea how much she hated all of this, the begging and always worrying about money. She started singing with him when she was too little to know better, and now she didn't have the heart to tell him how much she hated it.

"Look," he said. "It's a tomato-onion frittata."

Papa always took her with him, whatever he

did, wherever he went. He'd never leave her with anyone else. Which was probably why he started singing in the street in the first place, so he could keep Anna safely by his side. When she was little, Anna soaked up all the words to the songs and every once in a while she'd join in. When she was eight, she asked if she could pass the hat. Since then, she'd been part of the act. When it started out, she thought it was a game. But it wasn't a game anymore. That awful man was right. Papa should get a real job. She'd had that same thought many times herself. But Papa was so set on his life of "freedom." Whenever she brought up the subject of a real job, he made jokes and wriggled his way off the topic. It was just like when she tried to ask about her mother.

Anna took a bite of her omelet sandwich. She had been so hungry, but now Maria's good cooking tasted like straw.

There was no reason for Papa not to get a job. She was older now, old enough to be on her own if she had to. *She* was growing up. It was time Papa did, too.

IV

DAYDREAMS

Anna got up even earlier than usual to avoid riding the bus to school with Fiorella. She needed some time alone to think about how she could continue being Fiorella's friend and not let her find out about her street singing and the *pensione*.

The rest of the house was still asleep, except for Maria, who was always up before dawn. Anna collected her school clothes and tiptoed to the bathroom to wash and dress.

She turned on the tap—slowly—so it wouldn't squeak. The water ran out in a steady stream, filling the sink. The Signora only allowed them one bath a week. Anna made do with the sink in between. She washed herself, careful not to splash. The smallest noise could wake Signor Tomaso. Once, when they'd first come to the *pensione,* he'd planted himself outside the bathroom door, wheezing and talking at her. When she tried to escape, he blocked the way, talking faster, panting, and moving in closer. Finally, Papa had come to her rescue. Since then Anna was careful to be quiet.

Anna pulled on her blouse and skirt. No! There was a tomato-sauce stain on the skirt, her only school skirt. The spot wasn't very big, though Gina or Teresa would see it from a mile off. Maybe Maria could do something to fix it, mix up a potion or something. Anna gathered her books and schoolwork and tiptoed down the creaky stairs to the kitchen.

The room was steamy warm and smelled of bleach. Maria, who had a kettle on to boil, was dancing lightly in cloth slippers while stirring a large tub of laundry.

"*O quanto balle bene bella bimba, bella bimba, bella bimba. . . .*" Maria sang her nonsense rhyme very softly, so as not to waken the Signora. Her coal black curls bounced in time with her song.

"*Ciao,* Piccolina! You are up early today." Maria left off stirring her laundry, grabbed Anna, and waltzed her around the big oak table. They sang together in hushed voices, Maria in Italian and Anna in her own English version: "Oh, how daintily you dance, darling Dolly, darling Dolly. . . ."

"Do you have any dreams for me today, Little One?"

"Let me think . . . ," said Anna. Her dreams were fleeting pictures that faded quickly as she woke each morning. She closed her eyes and tried to remember. "There were birds."

"Birds!" Maria stopped dancing and released Anna. "What kind of birds?"

"Blackbirds, maybe. I'm not sure. They were high in the sky, flying away from me."

"Hmm." Maria frowned, creasing her forehead.

Anna shut her eyes again to see the birds more clearly.

"Now I remember!" The dream rushed back over her. "There was a big wave coming toward me. I looked up and saw the birds."

Maria crossed herself.

"Aye, Little One, this is a powerful dream."

Still frowning, Maria moved slowly around the kitchen, putting together breakfast. Anna kept still, her eyes following Maria's every move, her heart thumping away. Her dream might mean terrible things: blackbirds for death, the wave as a great flood of destruction. Maria had never been so serious.

Suddenly, Maria clapped her hands and

whirled around to face Anna, her black eyes sparkling.

"It is a *good* dream, Anna."

"Are you sure?"

"Aren't I always *sure*, Little One?" asked Maria, her warm hands on Anna's shoulders. "Great changes are in store for you."

"What changes? Maria, tell me more."

"All will be revealed in time."

Anna laughed and hugged Maria.

"You always say that. Can't you tell me something specific?"

"This I can tell you, Little One. You will need courage. Great changes demand that. The flying birds are a good omen. When the time comes, don't be afraid to fly with them. Now eat; I have work to do."

Anna sat at the table, slightly stunned. Maria's prediction was a little hard to take before breakfast. Maria brought her a bowl of yesterday's bread floating in hot, frothy milk, sprinkled with cinnamon and sugar. Anna stirred the bread. She had been wishing for her life to change for so long. . . . Maybe it could happen. Maybe this dream was the beginning of a different life. Maria knew these things—she could read dreams, cards, and even tea leaves. Anna shivered, remembering something Papa had said: "Be careful what you wish for; it may come true."

Maria twirled over to the table and dropped a large pat of butter into Anna's bowl.

"Don't tell," said Maria, putting on a stern look.

Anna crossed her heart. She'd never betray Maria.

"Eat now, Piccolina, while it is hot. Your destiny will wait until after breakfast."

Anna smiled and scooped up a sweet spoonful. She *was* hungry, and if she wanted to elude Fiorella, she'd better hurry.

Outside, the street was a cold, predawn pearly gray. Anna hugged her school satchel and ran toward Ponte Umberto, where she caught her bus.

The café-bars were doing a brisk business. People stopped for an espresso wake-up on their way to work. Only a few shops were open, not the fancy ones but places that sold olive oil or detergent. At this hour the shopkeepers were sweeping up, scrubbing their front steps, and setting out their wares. They were much too busy to notice her, though she passed them every single morning. A church bell chimed the hour. Anna held her bag tighter and raced for the 6:05 bus so she'd miss Fiorella, who'd probably be aiming for the 6:25. That was the bus Anna usually took, which got her to school in plenty of time for the eight o'clock bell.

She arrived at the bus stop warm and out of breath. Good! The number 280 wasn't yet in sight. She set her bag on the wall that ran along the river and watched the rising sun paint the angels pink on the Ponte Sant'Angelo, the Bridge of Angels. Castel Sant'Angelo, too, glowed rosy in the dawn's light.

The number 280 came rumbling down the *lungotevere,* the road that ran alongside the Tiber River. The bus stopped, the back door opened, and Anna grabbed her books and climbed on. She bought a ticket from the conductor and settled in a seat near the front for the long ride to school. The bus went on, stopping occasionally for one lone passenger. Buildings went by in a blur, and Maria's words came back to her.

"Great changes are in store for you."

Would she be changing schools? Maria said the birds were a good omen. So it would be something good; changing schools would stink. The other kids had finally stopped teasing her about being "the Stranger." They'd called her *la Straniera* as if being American was as strange as being martian. Only Fiorella had been a friend. If she left La Madama, she'd lose Fiorella.

Anna rested her forehead against the window, listening to the glass buzz. And suddenly it came to her. The impossible would happen! Papa would get a job! A good job, something like the one she'd invented for him, working for F.A.O. That was it! He could get a job *at* F.A.O. He would be the perfect person to work there. He'd traveled all over and he spoke English, French, and Italian. Of course they would hire him. The real miracle would be that somehow *he* would want to do this. He'd give up being a vagabond and start being a father, like Signor Mazzini. It was so simple. If Papa got a job, then she wouldn't have to worry about finding a new school because she wouldn't have anything to hide. Maybe once Papa got started on a normal kind of life, he might take them back to America, back to where they belonged, back home.

Anna sat up straighter, her heart racing. This was it, her dream coming true! All she had to do was tell Papa. Tell him . . . what? He'd like Maria's prophecy; great changes would appeal to him. But not if it meant *he* had to get a job. Could she tell him how much she hated street singing? How much she wanted a real home? Maybe it wasn't so simple after all. She looked down, and there was the tomato-sauce stain still on her skirt.

The bus pulled into Piazza Maresciallo Giardino, the end of the line. Anna raced off the bus, dodging the rush hour traffic to Via di Villa Madama, where the world became all at once filled with green. Her school was nestled against the dark cypresses of Villa Madama's park, away from the car fumes, where the air was sweet and fresh.

Anna ran through the front gate. She was part of the thin stream of early arrivals. Mothers walked their youngest to school: little girls in white smocks with black bows and little boys in blue smocks with white bows. Only the fourth and fifth levels got to wear jackets. It was good to be beyond the smocks; they looked so babyish. She greeted the old porter as she did every morning.

"Good morning, Mr. Giorgio."

"*Buon giorno,* Meez Amereeka," said Signor Giorgio, without looking up from his newspaper.

Anna hurried up the stairs to the second-floor washroom. It was so early, she had the sink and mirror all to herself. Her hair was a mess, sticking out every which way. She found her comb in the lint and grit at the bottom of her bag and dragged it through her ash blond hair, trying to smooth it.

Then she wet a paper towel and scrubbed at the stain on her skirt. It soon looked much worse than when she started. Hopefully it would dry out looking better. She tried fanning it and rubbing it with dry towels, which left paper lint stuck all over it. It was a disaster, and any minute someone was going to walk into the washroom. She twisted her skirt around so the stain was on the left side and hooked her schoolbag over her left arm to hide it.

Anna walked out into the hallway filled with kids. Fiorella and Teresa were standing by the classroom door.

"*Ciao,* Anna!" Fiorella came forward, all smiles, then stopped short, her face darkening. "I'm mad at you! Where were you? Babo walked me to the bus stop, and when you weren't there, he wouldn't let me ride here alone."

"I'm sorry," said Anna. "I didn't know. . . . I took an earlier bus. I—"

"So, we got the car," Fiorella went on,

paying no attention to Anna's lame excuses, "and he drove me all the way here, which was more fun anyway, except Babo kept saying it wasn't. But it was, especially after we picked up Teresa."

"Signor Mazzini was a riot," said Teresa. "He drove like a madman, leaning on the horn, cursing out all the other drivers. And *I* thought my brother could curse!"

"We almost ran into a bus," said Fiorella. "You should have been with us."

Anna laughed.

"Fiorella, you are such a *pazzerella,* a true noodle-head! If I had been with you, then we'd have been on the bus."

"Oh, Anna, you have to be with me tomorrow. Papa won't let me ride the bus alone. I don't want to have to change schools."

She didn't want to hurt Fiorella; she wanted to be her friend. It was awful all the secrets she had to keep.

"Don't worry," said Anna. "Tomorrow, I'll ride with you."

If only Maria was right about Anna's life changing. Then there'd be nothing she'd need to hide. Somehow she would convince Papa to get a job.

"Earth to Anna! Earth to Anna!" said Teresa. "Come on, Signor Amato's going to start attendance."

They filed into the classroom and took their seats. Anna, Teresa, Fiorella, and Gina sat together on the girls' side, next to the windows, at the front of the room. They'd started out at the back, but Signor Amato soon had moved them all to the front where he could keep closer watch. Anna tried to stay out of trouble, but Fiorella was always whispering something to her or passing notes. So Anna got her share of black marks, too.

Gina came flying into the room as the first bell rang and slammed into the seat next to Anna.

"*Ciao,* Anna. What happened to your skirt? It looks awful."

"Nothing. I . . ."

"Young ladies and gentlemen, quiet please. Class has begun." Signor Amato rapped his desk with a pencil, and slowly the class settled down.

Anna put the schoolbag on her lap, hoping it covered the stain, and pretended to hunt for a pen. Gina was waiting for an answer.

Suddenly Carlo and Salvatore, who sat in the front row opposite Anna, burst out laughing.

They'd seen her skirt! But how could they? She clutched her bag, feeling her face go bright red. No. It wasn't her, not this time. The boys were laughing at Fat Luigi, late as usual. Even wearing a uniform, he managed to dress funny. His pants were always too short, and today he had on lime green socks. Pretty soon all the boys and most of the girls were laughing.

She wasn't going to be a leper like Luigi, not if she could help it! She turned to Gina and hissed, "It's nothing. I spilled some water."

Gina mouthed an O and let the matter drop.

"Enough! Enough!" Signor Amato was getting worked up, his ruler smacking the desk. "Silence now, or black marks for everyone!"

The class hushed. There was only the sound of Luigi's corduroy pants legs rubbing together as he walked to his seat at the back of the classroom.

"Better," said Signor Amato. "Take out your homework. We'll begin with fractions."

Everyone groaned as they got out their homework. Fiorella tapped Anna on the back and launched a balled-up note over her shoulder and into her lap. Anna unwrapped it carefully, making sure Signor Amato's eyes were elsewhere. It said: *"Pranzo* at my house today. Say yes! (No excuses allowed. I already told my mother you're coming.)"

Anna shook her head. Fiorella had no problem asking for what she wanted. She didn't even bother asking. If only some of Fiorella could rub off on her. Maybe it would, today at *pranzo*.

The school day hummed along at a steady pace. After fractions they had grammar and then diction. At 10:30, midmorning break, Signor Amato lined them up and marched them downstairs and out to the playground. Anna's skirt had dried, and the stain barely showed. Once outside, Anna, Gina, Fiorella, and Teresa ran like mad to their hideout, part-way up the hill behind the school.

"Today," said Fiorella, dusting off the rock she always sat on, "Mama is making a special soup, *minestra* with chickpeas and gnocchi. Mmm-yum—*deliziosa!*"

Meanwhile, Gina and Teresa were getting settled on their tree stumps, unwrapping their morning snacks. Anna sat on a small flat rock near Fiorella.

"And then she's making a veal roast stuffed with sage and garlic."

All the talk about food was getting to Anna. She couldn't help it; her stomach growled like a sick tiger.

Fiorella laughed. Gina and Teresa exchanged a look that meant *la Straniera* is being strange again.

"Food for Anna," said Fiorella, unwrapping her snack. "Quickly, feed the starving American!"

Still laughing, she broke off pieces of bread and chocolate and handed them to Anna, Gina, and Teresa. Gina and Teresa shared their own snacks of biscuits, prosciutto, and white pizza.

Anna looked in her bag. Maybe Maria had given her some bread with olive oil she could share. No bread. But in the inside pocket was a pack of Brooklyn Bridge gum, her favorite brand! This was Papa's doing. And it was perfect. He knew they loved gum more than anything. *And* he knew it was strictly forbidden at La Madama. Anna held it up for the others to see.

"Gum!" said Fiorella. "Fantastic!"

"Two points for *l'Americana!*" said Gina.

Anna divvied up the pack. They each got one and a quarter pieces. But she made sure Fiorella's quarter was the biggest. They gobbled their snacks, saving the gum for the second half of lessons.

The warning bell rang, and they raced to join the end of the line of kids on their way back to the classroom.

After break was a lesson in geography. Signor Amato pulled down a blank map of Europe. As he pointed to the different countries, the class was supposed to fill in the country's name and capital. Anna knew them all. She'd been to most of Europe with Papa. On a map of the United States, the only place she'd be sure of was Willow Springs, Missouri. It was her birthplace, her mother and Papa's hometown. She had looked it up once in the library and spent a long time memorizing its exact place in the middle of America, her very own heartland.

"Anna," said Signor Amato, pointing to the center of the map.

"Will—" Just in time she stopped herself from blurting out "Willow Springs, Missouri."

"Czechoslovakia," said Anna, clearing her throat. "Capital: Prague."

Signor Amato nodded and called on Mario.

"Willow Springs, Missouri" would have had them in stitches. It would have become the new class joke, one they'd never let her forget. A little slip like that and she would wind up like Fat Luigi. She had to be more careful, much more careful.

V

CONFESSION

The final bell of the school day rang at 12:30. Anna and Fiorella raced each other to catch the bus. They got there just as the number 280 pulled away, leaving them with a ten-minute wait until the next bus.

"Why don't you call your father now and tell him you're coming to my house?"

"Sure," said Anna. "But I don't have a telephone token."

"No problem," said Fiorella. "I've got a *gettone*."

Fiorella led them to a pay phone at a café-bar and handed Anna the telephone token. But Anna had never used a pay phone, and she didn't remember the number of the *pensione*. Could she fake it? Not with Fiorella standing right in front of her.

"I can't remember the number."

"You really are a *stupidina*," said Fiorella.

"Don't you have it written down somewhere?"

Fiorella was right; Anna was a *stupidina*. The number was written on the inside flap of her schoolbag. Okay, she had the number, but she still didn't know how to make the call.

"You're right," said Anna. "I've got the number here." She opened the bag and folded back the flap. "But I can't call."

"Why not?"

"Please don't laugh. I really do feel stupid."

"What is it, Anna?" Fiorella looked serious and kind, like someone who could be trusted.

"I don't know how. I've never used a pay phone."

"Silly," said Fiorella, but she didn't laugh. She took back the token. "Tell me the number."

She dictated while Fiorella dialed. Then Fiorella held the receiver so that Anna could hear it ringing. Maria answered the phone. Thank God it wasn't the Signora. Fiorella deposited the coin, pushed the release button, and poked Anna to talk.

"Hello, Maria. It's me, Anna."

"Little One, are you in trouble?"

"No, I just want to ask Papa if it's all right for me to eat dinner at my friend's house."

"He's out getting a newspaper right now.

But I'm sure he wouldn't mind. He'll be glad you're getting something decent to eat for a change." Maria laughed. In the background the Signora was screaming.

"Tell me your friend's number, Piccolina, and don't worry."

Fiorella held up her own schoolbag, where the phone number was neatly written on a pink label. The Signora was getting louder and louder. Anna had to shout so Maria could hear her.

"I have to go now," yelled Maria. *"Buon appetito!"*

"Thank you," shouted Anna. "Good-bye."

"There," said Fiorella. "That was easy, wasn't it? Now tell me what was going on at your house. Who was screaming?"

"Nothing," said Anna. "It was just some crazy lady."

"She lives with you?"

"Sort of. She just . . ." What could she say? "She sort of manages things."

"And who were you talking to?"

"That was Maria," said Anna. "She cleans."

"Aye, you Americans!" Fiorella smacked her forehead. "You have a housekeeper *and* a maid! It's too much!"

"It isn't really like that." How weird for

Fiorella to think she was rich. But there was no way she'd tell her that they boarded at a *pensione*.

"Let's go," said Anna, "or we'll miss the next bus."

"Okay, Meez Amereeka. After you." Fiorella curtsied.

"Fiorella, stop it!" Anna pulled her up, and they ran back to the bus stop and climbed onto the number 280 just before it pulled away from the curb.

The bus was crowded, but they found two seats once they pushed past the mob around the conductor's stand. At least going into the city center the roads were fairly clear, not like the horn-blowing snarl of cars heading the opposite way, trying to reach the suburbs in time for *pranzo*.

Fiorella was quiet the whole ride back to the center, so different from her usual chatty self. She had been really nice about the pay phone. Gina or Teresa would have given her a hard time *and* not forgotten it. If she told her the truth about her life, maybe Fiorella could help her figure out a way to get Papa to change— *if* she could trust Fiorella with the truth.

The bus dropped them in front of the Palazzo

di Giustizia. They crossed the bridge, heading back toward Piazza Navona.

"So where is your new apartment?" asked Anna.

"It's an awful address," said Fiorella. "Don't you dare tell Gina or Teresa. It's on Via dei Coronari."

"I don't get it."

"It's where they used to examine all the corpses."

Coronari—corpses—street of coroners.

"I see what you mean. It is pretty gruesome."

"Where do you live?" asked Fiorella.

"On the other side of Piazza Navona." Anna waved her arm, taking in half of Rome.

"What's the name of your street?"

"Via dei Cornacchie," said Anna. It was easy to be vague but hard to tell a direct lie.

"Another ill-omened address," said Fiorella.

"I thought *cornacchie* were some sort of horns," said Anna.

"No, they're the blackbirds that eat carrion."

Crows! How strange living somewhere and paying no attention to its name. When she started learning Italian everything was such a mystery, it gave her a headache trying to understand it all. Many words she let slip by, never bothering to reclaim.

"This way," said Fiorella. She took Anna down a side street to a plain, mud-colored building. The entry was wide open.

"There's supposed to be a lady porter who watches the door," said Fiorella, "but she's usually sleeping."

They climbed up a wide, dark marble stairway. The walls were filthy, in need of paint and, in some places, plaster. This didn't seem like the type of building the Mazzinis would pick for a new home.

At the second-floor landing, the walls had been freshly whitewashed. The floor was swept clean, and a bright light shone over the doorway. Fiorella leaned on the doorbell. There was the sound of shoes clattering on marble, and the door was flung open by Fiorella's two younger brothers.

Fiorella dropped her schoolbag, tackling the nearest boy. Soon he was shrieking and wriggling, trying to get away from her. The other boy tickled Fiorella and his brother. The marble hall rang with their shouts and laughter. Signora Mazzini came running down the hall, waving a spoon and flapping a dish towel.

"Enough! Enough! Calm yourselves!" She slapped at her children with the dish towel, muttering an oath or a prayer, then took Anna by the hand.

"We leave the savages to their sport," she said, smiling warmly at Anna. "Welcome to the madhouse."

She brought Anna into the kitchen where Signor Mazzini sat frowning at the sports section of the newspaper. He looked up at Anna.

"Ah, here you are! This morning we thought you'd fallen off the earth. I'm glad to see you didn't."

Anna felt her face turning red. "I'm sorry, I didn't know. . . . I'll be there tomorrow."

"Now, now, not to worry. I hope you're hungry. Fiorella, Carlo, Salvatore! In the kitchen, NOW!"

Fiorella and her brothers arrived in a stampede.

"Wash up and sit down," said Signor Mazzini. "Our guest is hungry."

Fiorella gave her father a quick, strangling hug and a peck on the cheek. "Yes, Babo, right away."

Anna lined up at the sink with Fiorella and her brothers, who squirted each other with water. The kitchen smelled of all the wonderful things Fiorella had described. Anna hoped her stomach wasn't going to growl again.

They crowded around the table. Anna was seated between Fiorella and her father. Signora Mazzini began ladling a thick *minestra* into their bowls. The boys squirmed in their seats as they aimed kicks at Fiorella. Signora Mazzini served herself and perched on her chair. She made the sign of the cross, and there were two seconds of stillness as they all murmured grace.

Signor Mazzini passed Anna a bowl of grated cheese and spoke to Fiorella. "Did you properly introduce your brothers?"

"No, Babo, I will now. Anna, this worm is Carlo." Fiorella nodded to the boy opposite Anna. "And that worm is Salvatore."

"That is apt," said Signor Mazzini. "But not very flattering. Anna will think you don't love your brothers."

"I love them as much as anyone ever loved two worms," said Fiorella, and she dodged a piece of bread thrown by Salvatore.

"That's enough!" Signor Mazzini was serious.

Fiorella and her brothers settled down to inhaling their soup. Anna had been trying not to swallow hers in one gulp. It was so good, so much better than anything they ate at the *pensione,* it was hard to mind her manners.

"So, Anna, Fiorella tells me your father works for the F.A.O. A fine organization! What is his speciality?".

Anna choked on a spoonful of beans and pasta. She was coughing and gasping for air. Signora Mazzini rushed to her side. She patted her gently on the back and ordered Fiorella to bring a glass of water. *"Subito!* Right now!"

How could she! It was so embarassing. And what was she going to tell them about Papa? "I'm so sorry, I . . ."

"Sorry, for what? Are you all right now?" Signora Mazzini gave her a quick hug and returned to her seat.

"You should have pureed the soup," said Signor Mazzini. "How many times have I said this? A chickpea is a dangerous thing. If you kill a little American girl with your soup, you'll be starting the next war."

Anna wished she could slide off her chair, out the door, and down the stairs. These people were so nice, and she was causing all this trouble.

Fiorella burst out laughing.

"Babo, stop it! You're making Anna nervous."

"No, no, no. Anna knows a good joke when she hears one."

"*If* she hears one," said Signora Mazzini.

"All right, all right." Signor Mazzini turned to Anna and held out his hand. "Please accept my apologies for making a bad joke."

It was as dizzying as a roller coaster. She took Signor Mazzini's hand and managed a smile.

"That's better," said Signor Mazzini. "So wife, since your chickpea plot has failed, are you trying to starve us?"

"Now what?" asked Signora Mazzini.

"There is only soup for *pranzo?*"

"*Madre Dio!*" she said, rushing over to the oven. "Mother of God—the roast!"

Fiorella started clearing away the soup bowls while her mother arranged the meat and roast vegetables on a platter. It was a feast beyond anything Anna had ever had at Pensione Auriga.

Signora Mazzini put the platter in front of her husband, who began carving. Anna had seen this dish at the restaurants. It was veal rolled and filled with chopped herbs and prosciutto. Each slice had a savory, dark spiral set in the pale meat. Once everyone was served, Anna took a bite. This was better than anything she'd ever tasted, better than anything she'd ever imagined tasting. She sighed deeply.

"You like it?" Signora Mazzini was looking at her, slightly puzzled.

"This is so good," said Anna. "I don't know the words to say how good it is."

"Eat your fill," said Signora Mazzini. "That is the only compliment I need."

Only an occasional request for bread or salt interrupted the contented quiet as they devoted themselves to the roast. After seconds and thirds, Signora Mazzini brought a bowl of blood oranges, grapes, and nuts to the table. Carlo and Salvatore fought over the last orange. Signor Mazzini settled the argument by eating it himself.

Anna was dying to see what a real home looked like; she'd been inside so few of them. Would it be too pushy to ask for a tour?

"Fiorella, will you show me the rest of your apartment?"

Fiorella looked stricken. It was the wrong thing to ask, and it couldn't be taken back.

"What an excellent idea," said Signor Mazzini. "Help your mother with the dishes, and then show Anna your new home."

"Yes, Babo," said Fiorella, still looking upset.

They cleared off the table and helped with the washing up until Signora Mazzini shooed them out of the kitchen. Anna just barely remembered her manners.

"Thank you, Signora Mazzini, for inviting me to this wonderful meal."

Signora Mazzini smiled at her.

"Anna," said Fiorella, "relax. Come on, let's go."

Fiorella showed her a crowded living room, a small dining room piled with books, serving as an office for Signor Mazzini, and a bedroom Fiorella shared with her brothers.

The apartment was nice. Everything in it was spotless and orderly. Yet it was less than Anna expected. The rooms were all small, clogged with furniture, and dark. The room Fiorella shared with her brothers was so packed that two dressers had been put out in the hall, nearly blocking off the doorway.

Fiorella studied Anna's face and bit her fingernails as they went from room to room. Her nervousness was catching. Anna followed, tongue-tied, until they came to Signor and Signora Mazzini's bedroom.

"Oh!" said Anna, as they walked in the door.

The furniture was dark and carved all over with grapes, cupids, flowers, and graceful birds. There was a giant armoire, a chest of drawers, and a huge bed, taking up nearly all of the floor space. The bed was made up in white linens with lace pillowcases. Sitting atop the piled-up pillows was a porcelain doll dressed as a bride in white satin and lace. On the dresser was a silver-framed picture of Signor and Signora Mazzini on their wedding day. The Signora looked as pretty and fragile as the doll on the bed.

"It's so lovely," said Anna.

"Do you really . . . ?" Fiorella smiled and took Anna's hand.

"You're lucky," said Anna. "This is a wonderful home." She'd give anything to live in such a place, to have a real home. Maybe if Papa could just see it, he'd . . . Papa! He was probably wondering about her now. She had better get back to the *pensione*.

"I should go," said Anna. "Papa will be expecting me."

"So soon?"

"Yes, I have to. I wish I could stay longer. I really like your family."

"I'll walk you downstairs," said Fiorella, looking worried and sad.

They went into the kitchen, where Anna said good-bye to Fiorella's parents and brothers.

Signora Mazzini gave Anna a big hug and kissed her on each cheek.

"Come again," she said, looking straight into Anna's eyes. "Come soon, come often."

On their way down the gloomy stairwell, Fiorella pulled Anna to a stop.

"What is it?" asked Anna. Fiorella looked so upset.

"Can you keep a secret?"

"Yes," said Anna.

"If anyone from school found out it would be very bad."

"You can trust me," she said.

"I do trust you," said Fiorella. "You're different from the others."

"Yeah, I know. I'm a 'strange' American."

"That's not it. Or maybe it is. I need a friend. I need to talk to someone."

"Talk to me," said Anna. "What's wrong?"

"Our home—this apartment—is different from our house in Villa Madama." Fiorella was having a hard time getting the words out. Anna kept still, letting her take her time.

"We had to move here. Something terrible happened to my father."

"I'm sorry," said Anna. Fiorella still wasn't making that much sense. But she looked so miserable, Anna wished she could make her feel better.

"Babo had a store. Things went wrong with it. I don't understand quite what happened, but he lost money. He borrowed money from my uncles to help fix it, and he lost that money, too. And finally the bank took the store away from him."

Anna reached out for Fiorella's hand.

"It's a terrible, terrible thing. Mama says we are lucky because they couldn't take away our house. But we had to sell it to pay back my uncles. And then we came here to live. I don't want anyone from school to know anything about it. Please don't tell Gina or Teresa how small our apartment is or anything about this dirty old building. Please pretend that it's nice."

"Oh, Fiorella, don't worry. I will never say anything to hurt you. I'm very good at keeping secrets; yours will be safe with me." She squeezed her friend's hand.

"Anna, I really wanted you to see this apartment. I wanted you to know all about me. But you're so rich and this place is so ugly. I got worried. But you do understand, don't you?"

Poor Fiorella. It was awful to be so worried.

Funny that Fiorella was ashamed of a home that looked like a palace compared to Pensione Auriga. She wished she could share her own secrets with Fiorella. Maybe someday she would.

VI

THE EYE OF GOD

"Wake up, Anna-Banana. It's Sunday!"

Anna kept her eyes tightly shut while struggling out of her murky dreams to this rude awakening. Since she had had *pranzo* with Fiorella's family two days ago, Papa had been acting quite differently from his usual drowsy self. But this was really strange, for him to be waking her!

She kept quiet, hoping he'd go away. This was the only morning she could sleep in, and she wasn't going to give it up easily. Anna heard Papa cross the room and sit down on his bed. Good, he'd given up. She snuggled deeper into her pillow. When Anna had returned from the Mazzinis', she'd told Papa all about her visit. At first he seemed interested. But the more she told him, the less he listened. So she stopped talking about it. After that he started cracking more jokes, telling more stories, talking about new countries they should see and things they should do. He'd been throwing so many new ideas at her, as if he was trying to keep her too busy to think about the Mazzinis.

"Lazy Anna, will you get up, will you get up, will you get up?"

Now he was singing a nursery song! Papa's voice was pitched teasingly low, just loud enough for her to hear. She peered at him through half-closed eyes.

Papa was dancing with his guitar. He led it like a reluctant partner, swirling around the room, up and over his bed, dipping and twirling it. He stepped high on his stork legs, with his bare feet turned out like a duck. He had never looked sillier. She shut her eyes tight, trying hard not to giggle.

"Lazy Anna, will you get up? Will you get up today?"

It was no good; she couldn't fake sleep a moment longer. Knowing Papa was dancing around the room like a madman was worse than being tickled. She looked out from under her lashes, waiting until he was only a few feet away. And then she bopped him with her pillow.

Papa slumped to the floor, clutching the

guitar with one hand and his chest with the other.

"Hit in the heart!" He gasped, simulated a death rattle, then flopped back on the floor, still as stone.

She could hardly believe her eyes. Papa certainly had his funny moments, but she'd never seen anything like this before. It was so odd, she wasn't really sure it was funny.

"So, Anna-tutta-Panna, are you ready to rock and roll?" He got up off the floor, rubbing his knees. "We've got places to go, domes to see. Time's awastin'."

"Papa," said Anna, "are you all right?"

"Never felt better. What about you? Can't get out of bed?"

"I always sleep late on Sunday. It's the one day I don't have to go to school."

"It's after eight. That's late enough. Come on, Anna, don't be a grumpus. I've got the whole day planned. We have to get going so we can fit it all in."

"All right, I'll get up. But it isn't fair."

She got out of bed, feeling as rumpled as her pajamas. At the armoire she took out her favorite clothes: a pair of jeans that were soft as flannel but *not* ratty looking, and a sweater striped like a muted rainbow. She picked out clean underwear and took her clothes to the bathroom.

She felt better once her face was washed, and more interested in what Papa had planned for them. What did he mean by "domes to see"? Papa knew so much about Rome. Every so often he took her on one of his "fifty-cent tours." He'd taken her to the capitol hill at night to look out over the spotlit ruins of the Forum. By day, the Forum looked like a jumble of old stones and weeds. But at night it was magical, with the old white marble softly glowing and Papa crooning stories of the vestal virgins, senators in togas, temples, battles, and emperors. Anna shivered. She hurried into her clothes and back to Papa, ready for whatever he'd planned.

"Now that you're functional," he said, "the next step is to cadge a picnic lunch out of the Signora."

This should be interesting. The Signora was not likely to give up anything without a fight, especially where her food stores were concerned. But Papa could be quite persuasive, and he didn't give up easily, either.

Signor and Signora Rossi sat at opposite ends of the dining table, over the crumbs of their breakfast. Signor Rossi was lighting up his second cigarette since Anna and Papa had been in the room. Other than that, he was motionless, hardly there at all. Only a few of the boarders took advantage of the Signora's breakfasts of stale bread and bitter coffee. Those that did had left the table. The Signora stared at Papa, her face twisted in a look of disgust.

"But Signora Rossi," said Papa, as gooey as honey, "poor Annalina studies so hard. She spends all day going to school and doing her homework. . . ." He didn't mention the hours of begging at night. "What she needs is an afternoon of sunshine, fresh air, and the beauty of Rome."

"This is none of my affair," said Signora Rossi.

"My dear signora—"

"*I* am not your *dear* anything," said the Signora, brushing breakfast crumbs off her sunken black chest.

That was true enough. Anna bit the inside of her cheek to keep from grinning.

"Naturally, we'll be sorry to miss your delicious Sunday *pranzo*," said Papa. "We don't expect to have anything so grand for our picnic."

Now he was getting down to business. The Signora was interested, in spite of herself. If she could see their picnic as a way of saving on food and money, she'd go for it.

"All we need is some bread, a little cheese, an egg or two, perhaps . . ."

"That's enough, too much even! Maria! Maria! Come here!"

Maria just about fell into the room. When Papa had told her his plan, she planted herself outside the door so as not to miss a word.

"Si, signora."

Maria looked quite innocent, though rosier than usual. When the Signora looked away, Maria winked at Anna.

"You will give these two . . . ," the Signora said, indicating Anna and Papa with a flick of her hand, "two medium-size boiled eggs—*not* the large ones—two rolls, and a generous piece of fontina."

Maria turned brilliant red and seemed to be choking. Then Anna remembered that the fontina was a dried-out piece of cheese that Maria kept tossing in the trash and the Signora kept resurrecting.

"Si, signora." Maria could barely speak.

Anna, too, was about to explode.

"This is most kind of the Signora," said Papa. He was so solemn, so convincing, but then Papa didn't know about the cheese.

76

"It's nothing," said Signora Rossi, brushing away crumbs. *"Fa niente."*

"Thank you," said Papa, backing away from the table. He pulled Anna along with him, and as soon they were out in the hallway, they collapsed against the wall.

The next second Maria was out the door, racing to the kitchen. Anna and Papa caught up with her there. Maria was laughing so hard, she couldn't tell Papa about the cheese. Neither could Anna. Finally Maria went to the trash, rummaged around, and pulled out the rock-hard, mold-covered piece of fontina.

"Aha!" said Papa. "The generous piece of fontina."

They laughed until Maria was wiping tears from her eyes and Anna got the hiccups.

"Don't worry about the cheese," said Maria, pouring Papa a *caffè*. "I will fix you a fine picnic. It won't take long."

"What about the Signora?" asked Anna.

"The Signora will have a fontina omelet," said Maria.

"You'll get into trouble," said Anna. Maria shouldn't take such risks.

"It will be all right, Little One. The Signora only knows what she pays for, not what she eats."

In a short while, Maria handed Papa a string bag bulging with their picnic.

"Have a good day," said Maria. She draped her arm around Anna's shoulders. "Take a day off from worrying, Piccolina. Have *fun*."

"*Grazie mille*," said Anna, though a thousand thanks were hardly enough.

On their way out the door, Maria called after them, "*Fa niente!* It's nothing."

Papa led the way through the sedate Sunday streets, humming to himself. Anna followed, for the moment not caring where they were going. It was fun to joke with Papa and Maria about the Rossis, but they really weren't funny. The Signora was mean, so filled with venom. And Signor Rossi was so empty. How did people get like that?

Babies weren't like that, neither were kids, even at their worst. But there were plenty of grown-ups walking around, looking pinched and angry or all hollowed out. Bad things must happen to change people. Maybe one big bad thing; maybe lots of little bad things. She looked at Papa. Something bad must have happened to him. Could he become like Signor Rossi, a man shape with nothing inside? What about her? The begging made her feel angry and hateful, and every day the feeling grew.

What if she never had a real home? Would she turn out like Signora Rossi?

"Here we are," said Papa. "For the first part of our tour, 'The Domes of Rome.'"

Papa had brought them through a few short, winding streets to Piazza della Rotonda, the square that served as a welcome mat for the Pantheon. The Pantheon was one of her absolutely favorite places. It was the first monument Papa had shown her when they arrived in Rome. It was so close to Pensione Auriga that Anna had been to see it nearly every day since. So why did Papa wake her so early to see something she'd already seen hundreds of times?

"We've been to the Pantheon before," she said.

"True," said Papa. "But this is the fifty-cent tour."

"I hope it's worth two hours of sleep."

"I'll do my best," said Papa. "See the writing above the columns?"

"M. Agrippa, *L.F. Cos. tertium fecit*. You've already told me. It means 'Agrippa built this,' and he did it in 27 B.C."

"That's what is written," said Papa. "The truth is slightly different. Agrippa *had* built a temple for all the gods on this location. What you see, however, was built by Hadrian about one hundred and fifty years later."

"Then why did Hadrian say Agrippa built it?"

"That is open to speculation."

"What do you mean?"

"Your guess is as good as mine," said Papa. "The point is that something can be written in stone and still not be true. The real truth is what you carry in your heart."

Papa ambled across the square, paying little attention to the occasional car whizzing past. Anna trailed after him. Now what was he *really* talking about? He wove through the car park to an ornate marble fountain in the center of the piazza. The fountain held one of the obelisks the ancient Romans had stolen from the Egyptians. Papa sat on the step directly in front of one of the carvings. It was the face of a bearded man being cuddled by two sea creatures with pointy teeth. The marble man looked as if he were spitting at Papa.

"The dome of the Pantheon was originally covered with gilded bronze." Papa resumed the tour. "Can you see it, Anna, the gleaming golden dome set above sparkling white marble walls?"

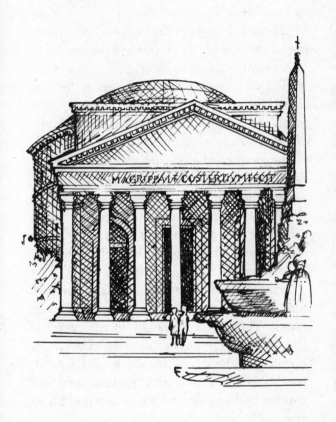

The Pantheon

Anna squinted, trying to see the dusty brick and marble as Papa described it.

"The columns were highly polished, showing off the gray and red veining in the granite."

A picture started to form.

"People from all over the Roman Empire came here to worship. It was a temple built for all the gods. Pilgrims climbed a wide flight of marble steps to the portico."

She envisioned men and women draped in flowing robes, soldiers in short tunics, and barbarians dressed in leather and furs.

"They strolled past the bronze doors into a sanctuary grander than anything they'd ever seen before." Papa's voice was nearly a whisper. "Come on, Annalina, let's go in."

Anna crossed the square into the portico's forest of columns and through the huge bronze doors. They walked straight to the center of the vast circle, to stand directly beneath the opening at the top of the dome. Papa stood, hands hooked in his back pockets, his head thrown back, talking up to the patch of bluest sky.

"The opening is called the *oculus,* which means 'eye' in Latin. It could be a window designed especially for the eye of God, which watches over us all."

His gaze suddenly shifted to her.

"Can you feel it, Anna?"

Her skin prickled. Of all the places she'd ever been, this felt most like a spot where God was watching. She looked up at the circle of sky, half afraid she'd see Him looking down from Heaven.

"The *oculus* is nearly thirty feet across. It lets in the light and air and, as you know, the rain."

Anna and Papa had run out to the Pantheon in many a rainstorm to watch a column of water cascade onto the marble floor.

Papa started walking around the rotunda, talking about niches and brick arches built within the walls to help support the dome. Anna walked one or two paces behind him as he explained the structure and history. His hair was as wild as ever and his clothes were rumpled. But Papa was so sure of himself and comfortable in his own skin, his clothes and hair didn't matter. He had his own dignity. Papa was being very thorough, going over every detail. But his voice was like a radio in a distant room. Her mind was on the *oculus*.

She had never thought much about God. It never seemed that He had much to do with her. Papa had shown her lots of churches and told her stories about Noah, Moses, the Virgin

Mary, and many saints, so that she'd understand what she was seeing. Those stories seemed like other people's fairy tales. Anna's fairy tales were all about her mother. The thought of God watching her was suddenly as magical as all the stories Papa told her about her mother, the magic swan. But this was better. God would last. Papa said that God watches over us all. Us all. She was part of that all. She belonged to God, and God belonged to her. It was as if a door had been flung open, and she was invited in. For once, Anna was inside with all the others, not outside looking in.

VII

PICNIC

How long had they been in the Pantheon? Minutes? Hours? Anna squinted against the sun's glare as they left the portico. It was hard coming back to this bright reality after the cool, gray depths of the Pantheon. Could God still be watching? Or was He blinded by the glare?

"On to part two of 'The Domes of Rome,'" said Papa.

"What? I mean, where are we going?" asked Anna.

"The Aventine Hill," said Papa. "And that's all I can tell you for now."

He paused a moment, looking thoughtfully at his sneakers.

"I'm sorry I woke you so early, Annalina. I thought this would be fun for you."

Anna studied her own faded blue sneakers.

"I'm not sorry," she said.

"Rome is so . . . I want to show you everything. Sometimes I get carried away."

"Papa," she said, taking his hand, "I'm glad you brought me here."

She looked up to see if this had sunk in. Papa smiled shyly and squeezed her hand.

"All right, then," he said. "Let's go."

They walked along, nearly touching, in the shadow of the Pantheon to Piazza della Minerva.

In the center of the square was a small obelisk set on top of a marble elephant. Most of the statues in Rome were so imposing and grand. She liked this one best because it wasn't that way at all. The little elephant seemed funny, all dressed up in a fancy elephant saddle, carrying the stone needle. His head was slightly cocked as if he were confiding to her, "Don't you think I'm a little bit silly?"

"Yes," said Anna, speaking out loud to the elephant. "You are silly. Isn't he, Papa?"

"Silly is as silly does," said Papa. "Since when do we talk to statues?"

"Since now," said Anna.

"Whatever you say. Bye, Elephant, catch you later."

He waved to the statue and ambled along the snaking street of ocher and umber toward the Aventine. Anna fell into step beside him. They walked slowly in the cool shadows, in and out of patches of hot, bright sunshine. Papa sang, "Swing low, sweet chariot . . . ," gliding from one street to the next. Anna could have followed him forever.

Everything had been so speeded up and crazy the past five days, with Papa acting strange and the kids at school thinking she was rich. It was good just to drift along. Since she'd told Anna her secrets, Fiorella had become her official best friend. They went everywhere and did everything together. If only she could trust Fiorella with her own secrets. It wore her out thinking up excuses for not inviting Fiorella to the "Palazzo Americano," as she had started calling Anna's home, the American Palace. Anna had told so many lies, and with each lie piled up on top of the one before, it made it harder than ever to tell the truth.

A Fiat came roaring down the street, blaring its horn. They flattened against one of the buildings until it passed. Papa grinned at Anna. Nothing bothered him. Well, today, nothing was going to bother her, either.

Pretty soon they were out in the open at Largo di Torre Argentina. The whole square was dug up to reveal the ruins of four ancient temples. Papa told her they were some of the oldest buildings in Rome. Now the temples were homes for hundreds and hundreds of cats. Every day old ladies brought them mounds of spaghetti on newspaper platters, the same way people in other places gave stale bread to pigeons.

"Here kitty, kitty, kitty," called Anna, trying to lure a little striped kitten out from the shadows of the marble ruins.

"Little Tiger, Little Tiger," Anna cooed, wiggling her fingers on the cold stone. The kitten lunged, and Anna caught him up in her arms and hugged him. He was such a soft little puffball.

"Look, Papa, he likes me."

The kitten was licking her hand with his raspy tongue.

"Anna," said Papa.

She knew. He didn't have to say anything. The Signora would never let a cat in the *pensione*.

"Good-bye, Little Tiger," said Anna, gently putting him down. "We've got to be moving along."

They left the piazza and were once again in the maze of medieval streets. After a bit, they came to the turtle fountain in tiny Piazza Mattei. Maybe it was "The Domes of Rome" tour, but Papa had included some of her favorite domeless spots. Four bronze boys each held on to water-spouting dolphins with one hand, and with the other they were boosting tortoises to drink in the fountain above. Papa stopped for a moment beside the fountain. He smiled; Anna nodded. They moved on, heading toward the river.

Drifting along, not speaking, they shared what Papa called "eye candy"—the synagogue, the ruins of Teatro di Marcello, and two small ancient temples. They crossed Piazza della Bocca della Verità with the sun high in the sky and the day grown hot.

Papa veered off to the left, up a steep, walled path through a park. Anna was climbing the Aventine Hill for the first time. Was there some huge domed church waiting at the top? All she could see were the dark, spindly cypress climbing up the hill. Anna was tired. They'd been walking for a long, long time. She wished they could stop in the park and cool off. Papa turned around to look at her.

"We're almost there," he said. "Are you okay?"

"Fine," she lied.

Eventually they came to a piazza surrounded by palm trees and cypress.

"This," said Papa, his arms held wide open, "is the perfect example of life imitating art."

They were in a hot, dusty square dotted with trophies and small obelisks. At that moment, she didn't really care about architecture. But there was Papa looking so excited, so eager to tell her.

"What do you mean?" she asked, trying to sound interested.

"Piranesi was a famous engraver. He designed this piazza to look like one of his own pictures."

"So, where are 'The Domes of Rome?'"

"Right this way," said Papa.

He waved her toward the massive gate on one side of the piazza. Anna approached it, looking for some sign of a dome. Maybe there was something hidden in the elaborate carving above the solid green doors. Though she looked carefully, all she could see were square crosses and symbols she didn't understand.

"What is this?"

"It's the Priory of the Knights of Malta," said Papa, "the residence of the Grand Master of the Order."

Dome of St. Peter's as seen from
the Priory of the Knights of Malta

What was he talking about? She was too hot and tired, not ready for the fifty-cent tour of the Knights of Malta.

"Come closer," said Papa.

He pointed to a small, round peephole in the door. Anna stepped forward and looked in. Through the peephole was a miniature scene as precious as the spun-sugar egg Papa had once bought her for Easter. Framed by the brass peephole was an avenue of trees grown together at the tops, forming a long row of arches. The pathway beneath them was striped with bands of sun and shade. And way in the distance, floating in a golden haze, was the dome of St. Peter's Cathedral. She had seen it a thousand times before, but never like this. Tiny and jewel-like, it was exquisite.

"Oh, Papa!"

It was so perfectly funny and beautiful. How could he know? How did he dream up "The Domes of Rome"? She loved him so much, it made her shy. She looked through the peephole at the miniature dome, afraid to move, afraid to disturb this happiness.

"Lunch?" asked Papa, very softly.

Anna turned away from the peephole to meet his gray eyes. She slipped her hand in his. They walked back down the sloping Via di Santa

Sabina to the walled garden they had passed earlier.

The garden was shaded with orange trees and high enough on the hill to offer a sweeping view of, perhaps, all "The Domes of Rome." Papa dropped the string bag on the grass in the cool shadow of the old fortress wall. Anna took out a flowered cloth and spread it on the ground.

The string bag held a feast. There were the eggs and rolls the Signora had grudgingly agreed to provide. There were also slices of mortadella and salami, a tomato-mozzarella-and-basil salad, black olives, and four blood oranges. Maria had even packed a small bottle filled with wine for Papa and one with mineral water for Anna.

"Maria has given us a miracle!" said Papa. "And to think it was only supposed to be two eggs, two rolls, and a rotten cheese."

"Maria can do anything," said Anna. "Difficult things get done immediately. Miracles just take her a little longer."

Papa uncorked their bottles and handed the mineral water to Anna.

"To our health! *Saluté!*" he said, clinking his bottle with hers. "And here's to the generosity of the Signora and the kindness of Maria."

"I'll drink to Maria," said Anna, "but the Signora . . . the Signora can eat her own fontina."

They both laughed and started eating. Anna piled mortadella on her roll and dipped it in the oil and juices of the salad. Papa handed her a napkin without comment and did the same.

Perched on the cool hillside, Anna could see nearly all the places they'd passed that morning. Only now she had God's view.

"Have you always known about the peephole?" she asked, helping herself to more salad.

"I discovered it during the summer," said Papa. "But then there were too many tourists. I wanted you to see it without having to push past too many cameras or wait too long in a line of cranky people."

"Can we go inside the gate?"

"I've tried to get permission," said Papa, "but they're very particular about who they let in. Being in the order would help, or having a bishop's miter."

"A what?" asked Anna.

"You know, those cone-shaped hats only the bishops get to wear."

"Then, I guess that leaves us out," said Anna.

"Good guess."

Papa peeled one of the eggs, handed it to

Anna, and then peeled one for himself. Maria even remembered to provide a pinch of salt, wrapped in its own neat paper packet. Papa salted his egg and took a bite.

"Wouldn't be a picnic without hard-boiled eggs," he said. "They are the very soul of a picnic."

"*Mmm.*" Anna's mouth was filled with hers.

"Seems like my mom used to boil up dozens for a picnic. She made fried chicken, too— heaps of it. From early in the morning, she'd be at the stove, her hair and eyes wild, tending three skillets of sizzling chicken and a big pot of eggs rattling on the fourth burner. Aunt Bessie brought the potato salad, baked beans, and a store-bought cake."

Anna kept still. If she was calm and didn't push him too much, Papa might keep on talking about Missouri.

"We'd all squeeze into Uncle Pete's station wagon and drive to a lake south of us. The boys sat in the way-back with the hampers and teased the girls 'til Uncle Pete slammed on the brakes, and that quieted things down for a bit."

"Who were the girls?" she asked, as casually as possible.

"Nellie and my three cousins. Sometimes a girl named Paula came. She used to talk all the

95

time about going to Europe, especially Rome."

Paula—a girlfriend? *The* girlfriend? No, Papa would never let her mother's name slip that casually. And Nellie? Was that Papa's sister, the oldest one? She chewed the last crust of bread, fingering a blade of grass.

Papa continued his story.

"Once at the lake, we were turned loose to do as we pleased. Uncle Pete and Dad unloaded the car, while Mom and Bessie took the little ones in the water. Then Dad hired a boat, rowed out to the deep water, and pretended to fish. Lou, Dave, and I used to swim out to him and dive down to tug on the lines just to keep him awake. He only caught us at it once.

"After we'd finished with Dad, we'd go into the shallow water and be sharks for the little kids, and then we'd tease the girls some more."

Papa laughed to himself. It sounded like the apple camp, only better.

"Then we'd eat up all that good food and laze about, almost too sleepy for mischief. After a while Dad got out his guitar and everyone sang the songs you and I sing now. Nellie had the sweetest voice."

Papa was looking at her. She must have been staring at him too hard. That's when he usually clammed up.

"Nellie has a girl your age."

"I have a cousin?" She could hardly believe it.

"Yep. You two used to play together as babies—that is, you used to maul each other. Of course, by now you probably have lots of cousins."

"You don't know?"

"Well, I sort of lost touch."

That was it. No more discussion. Anna could see it in his tightened jaw. He was even wiping his hands to be done with it. The end. But she wanted to know more. Didn't she have a right to these people, too? Weren't they her family as well?

Papa was tidying up, getting ready to leave. She couldn't look at him. A dam broke somewhere inside her and hot tears came rushing down her face, dripping onto the remains of the picnic.

"Anna, Annalina, don't. It was a long time ago. Now I've got you and you've got me. The rest doesn't matter."

He was holding her, drying her tears. It didn't help, not even a little bit.

"It does matter," she whispered. "It matters to me."

VIII

FRIENDS

It was Saturday afternoon, and Anna and Fiorella were squashed in the back of a packed bus, heading for home. The long school week was over. A day and a half of freedom lay ahead.

"So what are you doing tomorrow?" asked Fiorella.

She was fishing for an invitation again, and Anna was too tired to answer. A whole week had passed, and several times each day, she had to fend off Fiorella's attempts to wangle an invitation to the "Palazzo Americano." Anna had told so many lies and made up so many excuses, she couldn't keep them all straight. She'd been to dinner at the Mazzinis' twice that week, and it made her feel awful not to return the invitations. Fiorella had trusted *her*. Fiorella had never been mean. She was Anna's best friend. Didn't she have a right to know the truth?

Meanwhile, Papa was acting stranger than ever. Since the picnic he'd barely said a word to her.

"I have to go to mass with my family," said Fiorella. "After that, I'm free. I could come by and . . ."

"No," said Anna. "No! You can't. There's no place for you to come to."

"What?"

Was she really going to tell the truth? Now? She looked at her friend—her best friend. It was time Anna told her.

"There is no *palazzo.* Papa and I board in a cheap *pensione.* You think it's bad that your father doesn't have a job. It could be worse. *My* father has never had a job and *won't* get one. He's a beggar, and so am I."

"Anna, this isn't funny."

"You're right. It isn't."

"What do you mean, beggars?"

"We sing at restaurants and ask for money."

"You sing?"

"We both sing, and Papa plays the guitar."

"I don't believe you." Fiorella looked as if Anna had slapped her. "But what about your housekeeper and maid and your father's job at the F.A.O.?"

"I lied," said Anna.

"You lied to *me?*"

"I'm sorry," said Anna. "I didn't want to lie to you, especially about being rich. But one lie led to another, and it all got so tangled up. . . . I just didn't want to end up like Fat Luigi."

Fiorella's mouth was set in a straight, angry line. The next moment she was shaking with tears and laughter.

"I don't *believe* you!" she said, slapping Anna's shoulder. "You are such a *stupidina.* Fat Luigi! Oh, it is funny."

She could almost see the joke of it. Almost.

"Anna, don't cry!" Fiorella tugged at her arm, patted her back, and smoothed her hair.

She was such an idiot, crying like a baby on the crowded bus. People turned around to stare at her.

"I do understand." Fiorella spoke quietly, close to her ear. "It's like my father losing his business. I've been afraid of turning into Luigi, too."

Anna gave Fiorella a big hug right there on the bus, with everyone staring.

"But you didn't trust me," said Fiorella. "I'm not like Gina or Teresa. Couldn't you figure that out, Meez Amereeka?"

"I am sorry," said Anna. "I was too stupid and scared. Can we still be friends?"

Fiorella smoothed back her brown curls.

"Yes, but don't think I forgive you, because I don't."

"What?"

"Maybe later," said Fiorella. "First I am mad at you for being such a *stupidina*. Come on, this is our stop."

They fought their way to the door and off the bus. Once on the street, Anna felt too shy to look at Fiorella. Her secrets gone, there was nothing left to hide behind. Wordless, they walked down the street.

"So," said Fiorella, "what are you doing tomorrow?"

"I don't know," said Anna.

"Do you think you'll go on another picnic, like last week?"

"Papa hasn't said anything." Suddenly she had an inspiration. "We could go on a picnic, and you could come with us."

It was a great idea. Fiorella could see Papa at his best, and, finally, Anna could offer her a meal.

"Could I really?"

"Sure," said Anna. "We'll pick you up at your house around eleven."

"I could come—"

"No," said Anna. "You can't see the *pensione*. It's too awful. We'll come get you. Make sure it's all right with your parents. I'll call you tonight."

Fiorella gave Anna a squeeze.

"Hokay-dokay," she said.

"Okey-dokey," said Anna.

The picnic was a great idea, but how was she going to pull it off? Food would definitely be a problem. Maria couldn't sneak out enough for a third person, and it wouldn't be right to ask her to.

Best to buy some food. But what about money? Papa had just paid the Signora for the week, which left them pretty cleaned out. Tonight was their biggest night for tips, but that money had to stretch over Monday and Tuesday when tips were scarce. There was the money she'd been saving for a new coat. She'd borrow from that and pay herself back when she could.

Fiorella had stopped at her street corner. Now, she looked shy.

"If people pay you to sing, you must be good."

Anna shrugged.

"Sometime, will you sing for me?"

"Maybe," said Anna. "If you promise not to laugh."

"Never," said Fiorella. "Talk to you later. Don't forget."

"I'll call before six," said Anna. *"Ciao!"*

The picnic. What kind of food should she get? She'd like something as special as Signora Mazzini's feasts. What about Papa? What would he think about this? What if he didn't want to go on another picnic?

She was so busy worrying, she nearly forgot to turn and wave to Fiorella one last time. Fiorella was jumping up and down, blowing kisses. Anna waved.

What could she tell Fiorella if Papa said no? One problem quickly led to another. By the time she reached Pensione Auriga, she was sick with worry.

Most of the boarders were sitting around the table, waiting for *pranzo*. Anna raced up the stairs to their room. Papa was propped up in bed reading the paper. She dropped her school-books on the dresser, hung her jacket in the armoire, and went to the window. She couldn't look at Papa.

"Have the poor souls gathered for their meager repast?"

"Yes," she said, staring out the window.

"We should join the throng," said Papa.

Anna heard him sit up and hunt for his shoes.

"What's up, Banana? Why are you scrutinizing a blank wall?"

Her heart was racing. This was so stupid. Why was she afraid to ask him a simple favor? She turned around, still avoiding his eyes.

"I invited Fiorella to a picnic tomorrow."

Papa was silent. She felt him thinking no.

"I didn't know we were going on a picnic."

"Could we, please?"

"Okay, Anna. If that's what you want."

"I'll ask Maria to help me make something special to eat," said Anna. "Fiorella will really like your stories about Rome."

"Anna, it's okay. You don't have to sell me on it. Now, let's go down to lunch."

He said it was all right. But something in his voice said it wasn't. They walked down the stairs without speaking.

Downstairs, everyone was sitting in chilled silence at the big oval table with its patched linen. The Signora said that discussion interfered with digestion. Only Papa ever defied her. Even Signor Tomaso was hushed. Sometimes Anna liked the quiet, but today it was as leaden as their pasta and potatoes. She wished Papa would crack a joke or something to let her know he wasn't mad at her. But he didn't.

When Maria came to clear the table, Anna jumped up to help her, even though the Signora had said many times that it was vulgar for a "guest" to help a servant.

She felt safe the moment she stepped into Maria's steamy kitchen. She scraped and stacked the dishes, which Maria washed in a big soapy basin, rinsing them in another basin of boiling hot water. Anna dried and put the clean dishes back in the glass-faced cupboards. The whole process was like a gentle waltz.

"So, Little One, what are you doing tomorrow?"

"I can't believe I haven't told you yet," said Anna. "I asked Papa if we could go on another picnic and take Fiorella with us."

"How nice for you, Anna."

"We've got some extra money," Anna lied. "And I want to buy something special to eat. Will you please help me choose something and fix it?"

"*Si, si,* of course, Piccolina. We will make something very special." Maria took Anna's chin in her warm, soap-smelling hand. "Are you sure you have *extra* money?"

"Yes," said Anna, crossing her fingers behind her back. "We got thousand-lira tips from two Americans last night."

"We will make *vitello tonnato!*"

"Veal with *tuna fish?*"

"Trust me, Little One. It will be just right for a picnic."

It still sounded weird, but Maria looked pretty sure of herself.

"Where will we shop?" she asked.

"My friend Ersilia has a cousin who owns a butcher shop. We'll go in an hour, after *siesta.* You rest up until then."

"Okay," said Anna. She went up to her room, hoping Papa was already asleep.

An hour later, she slipped out of the room without waking Papa. He looked relaxed and happy. Maybe she was worrying over nothing. After all, he didn't say no to her plan. She tiptoed past Signor Tomaso's door and hurried downstairs to the kitchen.

Maria was waiting for her, dressed in her street clothes, a dark, striped dress worn with low heels and stockings. Her wild, curlicue hair was tamed by two gold clips, and a gold brooch was fastened at her neck.

"Signorina Maria, you are so elegant!"

Maria patted her hair and smoothed the skirt

of her dress. "Yes," she said, smiling. "I think it will do."

Anna handed her two thousand-lira bills.

"Will that be enough?"

"Plenty," said Maria. "Money will be left over." She tucked the bills into her worn leather purse and collected her shopping bag. They hurried out of the *pensione* before Signora Rossi could think of a reason why they shouldn't.

Ersilia's cousin's butcher shop was at the far corner of Campo dei Fiori. In the late afternoon, the large piazza didn't look at all like a "field of flowers." But every morning except Sunday, the square blossomed with flower stalls and fruit and vegetable stands. During the summer, Anna came here often to shop with Maria. Now the piazza was empty except for a few shreds of lettuce and the solemn statue of Giordano Bruno in the center of the square. He was burned on this spot for what Papa said was modern thinking but what the church called heresy. Burned alive! Anna shivered.

Maria flirted with Ersilia's cousin. In the end she got three veal cutlets and a can of tuna fish for only one thousand lira. On the way home she gave Anna the other thousand-lira bill.

"Put this toward a new winter coat," said Maria.

Anna felt herself blushing. Maria patted her hand and changed the subject.

"I think pasta salad will be good with the veal and perhaps some tomatoes. Is that all right with you, Anna?"

"*Mmm,*" said Anna, barely able to speak. "Fine."

Back in the kitchen of the *pensione,* Maria gave Anna an old, stained marble mortar and pestle and set her to work mashing the tuna fish into a creamy paste. Meanwhile, Maria prepared the veal and pasta. Anna ground the tuna slowly and steadily, adding olive oil, drop by drop, as Maria had shown her. Maria moved gracefully in the kitchen from task to task. Once again, they were caught up in their kitchen dance.

This was like her grandma getting a picnic ready in Missouri, boiling eggs and frying chicken. Maybe she was in her kitchen cooking that very minute. Grandma. Grandpa. Uncle Lou. Uncle Dave. Aunt Nellie. Aunt Nellie's husband must count as another uncle. Maybe her uncles were married now, too. So there were more aunts and, as Papa said, more cousins. That was just on Papa's side. Her mother must have had parents and probably sisters or brothers. In the middle of Missouri there was a huge family that she was part of and knew almost nothing about.

"Good work, Little One," said Maria. "It will soon be ready."

"Maria, tell me about your family."

"Haven't I already told you too much?"

"Tell me again," said Anna. "Tell me what it feels like having a family."

"It feels . . ." Maria's hands wove circles in the air, then she shrugged. "Sometimes we laugh or cry, or drive each other crazy. It is the same for you and your papa, isn't it?"

"Yes, but . . ."

"Perhaps some day you will find all of your family. But even if you never meet them, they are part of you and you are part of them. Meanwhile, you have your papa and your friends who love you."

Maria kissed Anna's cheek.

"Why doesn't Papa want to be with his family?"

"That is for him to answer," said Maria. "Someday he will tell you."

"Why does he act so strange about Fiorella? He seems angry that she is coming with us tomorrow."

"Ah, Little One, your papa is used to having you all to himself. Now that you are getting older, he has to learn to share you with your friends. Right now, he is a little bit jealous and, perhaps, scared."

"Scared?" What could he be scared of?

"He's frightened to see you growing up, knowing in the end it means you will leave him."

"I'll never leave Papa," said Anna.

"Piccolina, one day all children must leave their mamas and papas. Even Jesus Christ said it is so."

"I won't!"

"Someday, Anna, you will meet someone as wonderful as my Tonio, and you will fall in love. Then you will want to get married and have a home and family of your own."

"Oh, Maria, I want a *home* now. I want a family now!"

Maria pulled her close, gently rubbing her back.

"There, there, Little One. All will be well. Remember, great things await you."

DISCOVERY

Anna rocked in Maria's safe arms until Signora Rossi stormed into the room.

"What the devil is going on here? This is a kitchen, not a nursery!"

"I'm helping Anna prepare a picnic for tomorrow," said Maria, not a bit frazzled by the Signora.

"Picnic! The *Americano* has not asked permission. No, I've heard nothing about a picnic."

"It is a surprise Anna has planned for her papa. See, she bought her own veal and tuna." Maria was so calm. But then, she'd had a lot of practice dealing with the Signora.

"It may be her veal, but it's my oil and my salt!" Signora Rossi turned to Anna. "You steal my food, little thief!"

Anna cringed. Why couldn't she be as brave as Maria?

"And why aren't you making my supper?" the Signora shouted at Maria.

"Supper will be ready soon," said Maria.

"Well, get rid of the girl and see to it!" With that, she left the room.

"I'll finish up here," said Maria. "It's later than I thought. You'd better go get ready for tonight."

"All right," said Anna. She should have said more. At least, she should have said thank you, but the Signora had unnerved her too much.

Papa was sitting up in his bed, strumming his guitar, grinning.

"Hey, Anna-Banana, I've missed you. Whatcha been doing?"

Now that she was miserable, he was cheerful. Well, she'd try. "I've been shopping and cooking with Maria. She's been teaching me how to make something special for our picnic tomorrow."

"Great!" said Papa. He seemed to mean it. "Well, I'd best go grovel to the Signora."

"She already knows," said Anna. "She came into the kitchen while we were cooking."

"Poor Banana," said Papa. "That means she spoiled your good time."

Signora Rossi had called her a thief. "Yes," said Anna. "She did."

Papa got up and stretched. "All play and no work is making Papa lazy and poor. Let's get going."

"Okay," said Anna. "I'll go change."

Once dressed, Anna collected their snack from Maria and ran to meet Papa in Largo Giuseppe Toniolo. It was nearly six o'clock, time to call Fiorella. She asked Papa for a *gettone,* and they stopped at a nearby café-bar to make the call. Fiorella was even more excited than usual.

"Mama is helping me make a dessert," she said. "Eleven o'clock is fine. We'll be back from mass by then. See you tomorrow, Anna. I can hardly wait."

"Me, too!" said Anna.

"Have I ever seen you do that before?" Papa was pointing to the pay phone.

"No," she said. He noticed. "Fiorella taught me how."

"Oh," said Papa.

Was he impressed? Did he care? She was afraid to ask.

The evening went well for them. Piazza Santa Maria in Trastevere was thick with tourists. *Generous* tourists. Heading back toward Piazza Navona, they stopped at several restaurants in the narrower streets and small piazzas.

Papa liked these places best. In the summer, when there was always a bit more money, they'd eaten at a few of these small restaurants, or *trattorias*. Papa made friends with the owners and waiters. Now, when they came around singing, they were treated well. Often one of the waiters would bring a glass of wine for Papa and mineral water for Anna.

They crossed Campo dei Fiori on their way to a restaurant called Grappolo d'Oro, where they often had good luck. The square was lit by a three-quarter moon and two street lamps. Their shoes clattered on the cobblestones, much too loud for the hushed square. At night Campo dei Fiori belonged to Giordano Bruno. Moonlight silvered his head and shoulders; his sad face was completely lost in the shadow of his cowl. She stepped lightly so as not to disturb him.

The restaurant had a large, brightly lit sign of a bunch of golden grapes. They arrived just as a grizzled old Neapolitan was slamming his way through "O Sole Mio," accompanying himself on a wheezy accordion. Papa pulled Anna back into the shadows. It was a professional courtesy to keep back, out of the way, until another performer had finished his songs and collected all his tips. Anna sat down on a

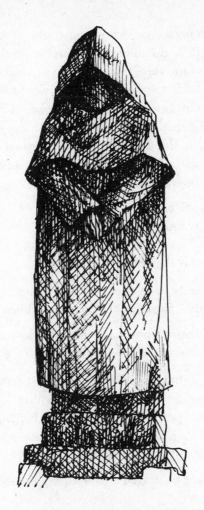

*Statue of Giordano Bruno
in Campo dei Fiori*

curbstone to rest while she could. They still had all the restaurants and cafés around Piazza Navona and the Pantheon to sing to before they went back to the *pensione*. It would be past midnight before she saw her bed. Thinking about it made her more tired.

When the Neapolitan was finished, Anna and Papa stepped forward. Papa strummed a few chords and began.

> In a cavern, in a canyon,
> Excavating for a mine,
> Lived a miner, forty-niner,
> and his daughter, Clementine. . . .

He only sang the first two verses of "Clementine," the ones that sounded funny.

> . . . herring boxes without topses,
> Sandals were for Clementine. . . .

He didn't sing the part about Clementine falling into the water and drowning. That is what happened to her in spite of her big feet. But it wasn't the kind of thing people wanted to hear, eating their dinner.

> I come from Alabama with my banjo on my
> knee.
> I'm going to Lou'siana, my true love for to
> see. . . .

She was glad to move on to "Oh, Susanna" and not have to worry about that miner once he'd lost Clementine.

> . . . the sun so hot I froze to death,
> Susanna don't you cry.

Then Papa began her favorite song. The song that belonged to her as much as anybody could own a song. He always sang the verse alone. It gave her goose bumps because it was so beautiful and so sad.

> Blackbird, blackbird singing the blues
>   all day,
> right outside of my door.
> Blackbird, blackbird, gotta be on my way,
> where there's sunshine galore.

Tonight, instead of being lulled into the sad, bluesy mood of the song, she felt as if someone had just poured ice water down her back. This song was one of Papa's stupid jokes! And tonight, for the first time, she got it. Via dei Cornacchie—Street of Crows. Street of Blackbirds. Papa had known this all along. Maybe that's why he sang the song at least once every night. It was his song, too. Maybe it was why he'd chosen Pensione Auriga in the first place—because it was haunted by the most mournful blackbirds in all of Rome. She caught his eye and he gave her the glimmer of a wink. Why hadn't he told her before? Papa started up the chorus and she joined in:

Pack up all my care and woe,
here I go singing low,
bye bye blackbird.
Where somebody waits for me,
sugar's sweet, so is she,
bye bye blackbird.

No one here can love and understand
   me. . . .

When Papa began the second verse, it was her cue to start passing the beret. But tonight she was too lost in the song to move an inch.

Bluebird, bluebird calling me far away,
I've been longing for you.

Had Papa been waiting for a bluebird to arrive? Had he been longing for it as much as she had?

Bluebird, bluebird, this is my lucky day,
now my dreams will come true.

"Wake up, Annalina," said Papa. "The song's over."

He smiled one of his saddest smiles and handed her the old beret. She took it and walked slowly from table to table. The song played on in her head. Would a bluebird be able to find its way to Via dei Cornacchie? Would she know one if it came? Would Papa?

"Please, dear, tell me your name."

Anna looked up. A round-faced woman with hazel eyes was searching her own. She hated this. Someone was always asking her name, as if she didn't deserve any privacy. Usually she lied, but this woman looked so . . . so honest.

"Anna."

"Ann! I had to be sure. Why you look just like her. It breaks my heart."

"What?" asked Anna. What was this woman saying? "I mean, who do I look like?"

"You look like Florry when she was your age," said the woman.

"Florry?"

"Your mother, Ann."

Her mother! Florry! A giant wave spilled over her and all else was blotted out by its roaring in her ears. *Florry*. Her mother's name. Papa had never been able to say it.

The woman reached out and was patting her hand. "Ann, are you all right? I'm sorry I frightened you. You gave me quite a turn when you first came out of the shadows. I thought you were Florry's ghost."

Ghost? Anna could hardly breathe. Suddenly, Papa was at her side.

"Hello, Paula," he said. "Anna, this is an old friend of mine."

"I'm not all that old," Paula said to her. "But I've known Stephen since we were babies. Florry and I were best friends. We all grew up on the same street."

Anna looked at Papa. Was this really so? Papa looked dead serious and pale. Talk about seeing ghosts. Her own heart was thumping against her ribs. Florry! She could hardly believe this. But it was true. It was happening.

"Well, Stephen, so we both finally made it to Rome, after all. But I guess you beat me by a couple of years."

This was the Paula he'd told her about. The one on the picnics—the one who wanted to go to Rome.

"Yes," said Papa, pulling Anna close against him. "We've been here a while."

"And other places, too?" said Paula. "Pull up a chair and tell me about it."

"Well," said Papa.

"Stephen, there's nothing to be afraid of. I'm here on my own."

"It's getting pretty late," said Papa. He was holding Anna tighter and tighter. "It's past Anna's bedtime."

What was he saying!

"Then come have an early breakfast with me tomorrow at my hotel," said Paula. "I'm leaving on a noon flight, but we could have plenty of time to catch up with each other. Willow Springs has changed since you've been gone, changed for the better. We've a lot to talk about, if you can manage to rouse yourself."

This woman really knew Papa. She probably knew exactly what had happened to her mother. And maybe Paula could tell her what had happened to Papa to make him so nervous about America. As far as Papa was concerned, Paula knew too much. He was shifting from foot to foot, his grip on Anna getting tighter.

"I don't think we can get together," he said. "Anna has made plans for early tomorrow morning."

"We don't have to pick up Fiorella until eleven," said Anna.

Papa shrugged and started drifting away. He wasn't even going to say good-bye. Anna turned to Paula, speaking quickly. "We could meet you before then."

"Good!" said Paula. "Spoken like your mother. Come to the Hotel Nazionale at eight. Do you know where that is?"

"Piazza di Montecitorio?" asked Anna.

"That's right," said Paula. "If you can't get him out of bed, you come along by yourself. I'll be waiting for you."

"I'll be there."

Nothing, but nothing, would keep her away from Paula.

"I'll be there." Then she turned and raced after Papa.

"Why did you lie to her!" Anna was breathless from trying to keep up with him.

He marched on, not answering, crossing Corso Vittorio Emanuele into the brightly lit Piazza Navona, and charging past the Saturday night crowds.

"I don't even *have* a bedtime."

"Anna, I know. It was just a white lie."

"But, why?"

"I don't want to hang around with Paula Simmons hashing over what was."

"Well, at least you can slow down," said Anna. "She's not chasing after you."

Papa stopped and looked at her.

"Annalina, let's sit a moment."

He rested his guitar on the pavement. They sat on the curb opposite Fakiro, who had gathered a large crowd to watch him swallow swords and flaming torches.

"Was my mother's name really Florry?"

"Um."

"Was it?"

"Florry-Dorry, to me," said Papa. "Her real name was Floren Alice Decker."

"And you grew up on the same street?"

"Yep."

"And?"

He looked tired.

"Anna, I really don't want to talk about it."

"I need to know."

"It's all in the past. It's over," he said.

"Papa, please?"

She held her breath—afraid he wouldn't tell her, afraid he would.

There was a long pause. Papa studied the ground, rubbed the stubble on his chin, and began.

"Florry and I got married kinda young. Nobody approved of it. Her parents were dead set against it. Mine weren't too pleased. It was a big . . ." Papa's hands shaped the air, then crumpled into fists. "Well, they got over it.

Mostly because my mom kept her head and didn't let the gossips get to her. Then you came along and everyone started speaking again."

He began worrying a spot on his pants leg.

"And we were happy. Then she died."

She died. But how?

Papa was rubbing at the spot, erasing it with his fist.

"There was an accident. The motorcycle hit ice. Florry was thrown off and died."

Anna felt a pain in her chest, a hot stab of truth.

"You never told me. You never even told me her name."

"No," said Papa. "I didn't."

Didn't she have a right to know? After all, she was her mother.

"Were you there?"

Papa nodded.

"I wished I'd died with her." He put his head in his hands and talked to the paving stones, his voice hoarse and choked sounding.

"Everyone went crazy. Your grandparents started fighting about who was best suited to take care of you. Even Nellie got into the act, saying she could raise you with her own little girl. So I took you away before they could."

They sat, silent as marble, while the Saturday night crowds of Piazza Navona passed them by.

"Do you understand?" he asked.

"Yes," she said. But she didn't understand, not one bit of it. Her grandparents wanted to take her away from him? How could anyone take her away from Papa?

"Let's go home," he said.

Home! Her heart leapt to her throat. But no, he just meant the *pensione*. Her mother was gone. Home was gone. Papa left it to keep her with him.

He pulled her gently to her feet and kept her hand tightly in his all the way back to Blackbird Street.

X

BREAKFAST WITH PAULA

Anna opened one eye. It was finally seven o'clock, according to Papa's watch on the pillow beside her. She got up so many times during the night to check on the time that eventually at four in the morning she moved the watch to her pillow. When she wasn't worrying about her breakfast with Paula, she was going over the story Papa had told her.

It had been impossible to sleep, and now she was exhausted and nervous about the morning ahead. Papa was a softly snoring lump under his covers. Before they turned in for the night, he had made it clear that he wouldn't join her for breakfast with Paula.

"I just don't want to see her. Paula Simmons is part of a past that I don't want stirred up. If you must see her, do. But don't get carried away with small-town gossip."

She didn't want to upset Papa. But she

needed to find out more about her mother. She needed to know about Willow Springs—about her family there and the home she'd had and lost—all the things Papa couldn't or wouldn't tell her. This might be her only chance.

She sighed, slid out of bed, and went to the bathroom to get ready. She put on her school skirt and the rainbow sweater, then scrubbed her face and pulled at her hair with a wet comb. She'd try to make up for last night when Paula had seen her looking like a beggar.

Not that Paula appeared to notice how she was dressed, or paid much attention to what she and Papa were doing. Paula seemed to look through all that and simply see Anna. Or perhaps it was Florry's ghost she had her eyes on. Anna looked at herself in the mirror. Did she really look just like her mother?

She tiptoed down to the kitchen. As usual, Maria was busy working.

"What is it, Little One? Why are you up so early?"

"I'm meeting an American lady who grew up with Papa and my mother. She was at one of the restaurants last night."

"Where is your father?"

"He won't come. He can't. Last night he told me about my mother. How she died."

"Anna." Maria smoothed the hair off her brow. "You didn't know before?"

Anna shook her head no.

"You will be all right, Little One." Maria hugged her. "You have grown up so well. You are such a lovely girl. I think your mother has been watching over you, all along."

Maria stepped back. "If you go see this American lady, will you still have your picnic?"

The picnic! She'd nearly forgotten.

"Yes," she said. "The picnic is still on. I'll come back soon and help you get ready."

"Don't worry about that," said Maria. "You need time to be with the American lady."

"Why does everything have to happen all at the same time?"

"I don't know, Little One, but that is the way of it."

Outside, the shops were shuttered, the streets quiet with an unmistakable Sunday stillness. A few women in rusty black dresses were marching toward the Church of the Maddalena for early mass. Anna arrived at the Hotel Nazionale just as the church bells pealed. The heavy door of gleaming brass and glass swung silently open as a doorman ushered her in.

The lobby was more elegant than anything she'd ever seen. Silky oriental rugs made pools of bright color on the dark polished floor. Plush chairs were grouped around tables laden with flowers. Paula emerged from a deep armchair and came to Anna with open arms.

"Oh, Ann, here you are! I'm so glad."

Paula held her a moment and Anna felt her own stiffness yielding to this warm stranger.

"I *never* thought I'd find you," said Paula. "I came to Rome because Stephen and I used to talk about it so much. And I looked for you everywhere. But I didn't believe I'd find you. How could I? It was such a long shot."

She held Anna at arm's length.

"There were no tricks in the moonlight," she said. "You look like Florry in the morning, too."

Paula led her to a sunny dining room where the tables were draped in white linen and pink roses spilled out of crystal bowls. The maitre d' led them to a corner table, wished them a pleasant meal, and glided off.

Anna perched on the edge of her chair, fingering the heavy silver spoon by her plate. She'd never been anywhere this fancy. Paula reached across the table and patted Anna's hand.

"I have to make sure you're real," she said, smiling. "Annie, do you want a real American breakfast with bacon and eggs? They can do that here, and the waiter doesn't even sneer when you order it. Would you like that, Ann?"

It was so strange. What she'd really like was to go back to Maria's kitchen. But she had to find out about her mother and Willow Springs.

"I'll just have rolls and coffee, please," she said.

"Coffee?" asked Paula.

"If that's all right," said Anna.

"Is that what Stephen gives you?"

Anna nodded. What was wrong with coffee? Paula motioned to the waiter.

"Two continental breakfasts," she said.

The waiter bowed ever so slightly and silently slipped away.

"Do I really look like my mother?"

"So very much," said Paula. "Doesn't Stephen tell you so every day?"

"He doesn't like to talk about her."

"I can't say that surprises me," said Paula. "But you must have seen pictures of Florry?"

"No," said Anna.

"It's worse than I'd thought," said Paula. "And probably why Stephen didn't want to come here."

"He has trouble getting up in the morning," said Anna.

"It's more than that, isn't it?"

"Well...," said Anna.

"Stephen has gotten so used to running away, that's all he can do."

"What do you mean?"

"The day after the funeral, Stephen packed his bags and you, and ran as fast and as far away as he could."

"Papa told me last night that my grandparents were going to take me away from him."

"They certainly ganged up on Stephen. At the time, I thought they were going to take you away, too. I even gave Stephen money to help him leave town. Since then, I've truly regretted my part in the Great Escape."

The waiter returned with silver pots of coffee and steamed milk and baskets of croissants, hard rolls, and sweet muffins. There were small crystal pots of jams and a plate of butter pats shaped like flowers. The food turned Anna's stomach. She just wanted to hear her parents' story.

Paula poured out milk and coffee for them and offered Anna a basket of rolls.

"If your father had stayed put for a while and toughed it out, everything would have been fine. Your grandparents aren't monsters. They didn't want to cause Stephen more grief,

and they certainly didn't want to hurt you."
Paula sipped her coffee.

"When Stephen left, it was as if you both had died, too. Your grandmothers were sick. Stephen's mother put ads in big city newspapers and sent letters to American Express offices all over Europe, begging your father to come home. A few years ago someone reported seeing you in France, but that was all they ever heard of you."

"That's when we were picking apples," said Anna.

"Were you happy?" Paula was staring at her.

"Yes." That time *was* happy.

"I've been so worried about you, losing your mother *and* your home."

But Papa had to run away. They were going to take her away from him.

"Worst of all is what it's done to Stephen, always running away. Well, there comes a time to stop running and face up to it."

"Face up to *what?*"

"Florry's death."

Paula put down her cup.

"Oh, honey, I don't want to upset you. Would you rather I didn't talk about your mother?"

"No. I want you to. . . . I want to know about them."

"They had quite a story. It was . . ." Paula bit her lip and smiled. "It was very romantic." She took a deep breath and buttered her croissant.

"As I said, they grew up on the same street, though they totally ignored each other until high school. Then Stephen got a motorcycle. One day he looked up from a gasket, saw Florry as if for the first time, and fell madly in love. Florry said it took her a bit longer."

"Longer for what?" said Anna.

"Longer to decide if she loved him. She said it was exactly seventeen and a half minutes. And that was that."

"Do people really do that? Fall in love so quickly?"

Paula shrugged.

"That's how your parents did it."

Anna tasted her hot milk and coffee. It sounded like one of Papa's fairy tales, only more confusing.

"Well, for some reason," said Paula, "everyone blamed Stephen, as if it were all his fault. Maybe because he had that motorcycle. Anyway, that was all nonsense. No one was to blame. They were simply in love. Please pass the jam."

Anna handed her one of the little dishes and tried to be patient while Paula helped herself and took a bite.

"Anna, you haven't eaten a thing. Do you want to order something different? Are you sure this isn't too upsetting?"

"No, yes, *no.* I just want to hear this."

"Right," said Paula. She put down her cup. "Your grandparents tried their best to keep Florry and Stephen away from each other. Florry's parents were particularly strict. But love will find a way."

"What do you mean?"

"Florry got pregnant her senior year and had to quit school."

"What!"

"Now don't think for one second that you were a mistake."

This was the most incredible thing in the world! Here was this woman she barely knew, telling her about *sex!* And it wasn't general sex, like birds and bees stuff, it was her very own mother and Papa. She stared at the tablecloth, feeling the blood rush to her face.

"The grandparents-to-be were furious. They threatened Florry and Stephen with all sorts of awful things. Florry didn't care. She was thrilled to be pregnant, couldn't wait to be a mother. Finally, your grandparents gave in and Florry and Stephen were married. They were set up in a dumpy little apartment over Baine's Hardware Store. And they settled in, as Florry put it, to live 'happily ever after.'"

This was harder to believe than the story of the magic swan. But she liked it better. Her mother sounded so daring.

"Don't you remember Florry the least little bit?"

Anna shook her head no.

"That is very sad. She was so bright and beautiful, and she loved you so much." Paula smiled at Anna. "You two had such fun together. Florry was like a little girl with her dolly. You all should have lived happily ever after."

"Papa told me about the accident."

"Lord, what a nightmare!" said Paula. "No one could make sense of the death of Florry. People needed to blame someone, and though it was absurd, they blamed Stephen. And they said such hateful things."

"That's not fair."

"It *wasn't* fair, but Stephen shouldn't have listened. Anna, your father has been running away from Florry's death and his own stupid guilt. Fear of losing you hasn't been the real issue."

It was! Papa had to . . .

"This vagabond life is terrible for a child. I don't know how Stephen can have justified it to himself for so long. It certainly isn't what Florry would have wanted for you."

Anna was hanging onto the edge of the table, digging her nails into the thick linen. Papa had always done what he thought best. He loved her. Paula couldn't understand that.

"I have to go now," Anna said, standing up.

"Oh, Annie, don't. Don't run away. I don't want to lose you again."

She could hardly think. She did want to run, as far away as possible. But if she left Paula now, she would lose her chance to know Florry. Very slowly, she sank back into her chair.

XI

GOING FORWARD

For the rest of their breakfast Paula told Anna stories about when she and Florry were growing up. The good times. If only there were a way to memorize it word for word, to save for later.

Sometimes, Florry and Paula were the girls Papa and his brother teased on the long drives to the picnics. It didn't surprise her that Papa had left Florry out of *his* picnic story. In Paula's version, Florry did more than her share of teasing the boys. Florry reminded Anna a little bit of Fiorella. She sounded so sure of herself.

"She used to boss me around," said Paula. "And I never minded because Florry always had a good plan, even if it usually got us in trouble."

"Like what?"

"Like borrowing shopping carts from the A & P to hitch up to your grandpa's hound dogs for chariot races." Paula laughed. "It was slow going until one of the barn cats happened by. And *that* got those dogs moving."

"There was a barn?" said Anna.

"Yes, a big, old rust-colored barn alive with mice, bats, barn cats, and children. There was a hayloft that was strictly off limits. And that's where Florry and I had our secret hideout." Paula laughed. "I loved that old barn; it felt so safe."

"Is it still there?" asked Anna.

"Oh yes," said Paula. "Your cousins have taken it over now. Of course, your aunt Nellie forbids it. But that doesn't matter; haylofts belong to kids."

"How many cousins do I have?"

"Nellie has three children, Lou has a boy and girl, and Dave has five. Florry's sister has twin girls and her brother, John, has a baby boy."

Anna kept count on her fingers. She had thirteen cousins! It was as big and complicated a family as Fiorella's or Maria's in Calabria.

"Does everyone still live in Willow Springs?" she asked.

"Mostly, yes," said Paula. "Dave moved to Denver with his brood. But they come back every year for either Thanksgiving or Christmas."

"Thanksgiving," said Anna. "Is that when you eat turkey?"

"You've never had a Thanksgiving, have you?"

Paula's look was filled with pity. It made Anna's heart race. She liked Paula and knew she meant well, but she couldn't stand being pitied by her.

"On Thanksgiving," said Paula, "there's about a ton of food: turkey with sausage stuffing, candied yams, cranberry relish, creamed onions, and apple, pumpkin, and pecan pies. Everybody brings something. In my family, I'm in charge of the Jell-O mold. The food is great. But mainly Thanksgiving is about families getting together."

Paula was giving her that look again.

"You should be part of it, Ann. It's your birthright."

Anna thought about all that weird food, though it probably tasted pretty good, especially the pies. And all those people who were *her* family. She and Papa should be there with them. It was what she'd always wanted. But right now, she didn't want Paula to see that wanting. Anna cleared her throat and changed the subject.

"Is my grandfather a farmer?" she asked.

"No, he sells insurance. Your great-grandfather Farrin used to run the farm. Now your great-uncle Pete has taken over and soon his son will be in charge."

"Is it like Dorothy's farm in *The Wizard of Oz?*"

"Not a bit," said Paula. "Though they keep a few chickens and a goat. It's mostly soybeans."

Paula looked at her watch.

"Lord, I'll miss my flight," she said. "It's awful to see you for such a short time. If I could stay longer, I would. My two weeks in Rome are up. But I *will* see you again."

Paula signed the check, and they left the restaurant. In the hotel lobby Paula took Anna's hands in hers.

"I'm sorry if I said anything to hurt you," she said. "I know Stephen thought he was doing right by you, but I think he was mistaken. Your grandparents still want you with them, Ann. They *miss* you. If your father won't bring you back home, you should come on your own."

Anna's hands were getting hot and sticky in Paula's grasp. She couldn't look at her.

"No one wants to harm you in any way," said Paula. "I'll send you photos of Florry and

Stephen the minute I get home. Just wait 'til you see her. She was"—Paula's eyes were bright with tears—"so much like you."

"Thank you for the breakfast," said Anna.

"Oh, Annie, you are the silly one, thanking me for a breakfast you barely breathed on." Paula hugged her tight and whispered, "Goodbye."

Anna ran all the way back to Pensione Auriga, clutching Paula's address in a tight fist, the streets blurred by her tears.

She tried to calm down as she climbed the stairs. On the second-floor landing, she sideswiped one of the little old ladies.

"Sorry," said Anna.

The old one looked at her with owl eyes, patted her hand, and shuffled off. She must have looked pretty pathetic. She'd better stop in the bathroom to soak her face in cold water. She didn't want Papa to see her with red, swollen eyes. She had to get him in a good mood for their picnic with Fiorella.

Papa was propped up in bed with his guitar.

"Hey there, Anna-Banana! How's it going?"

"Okay."

He hopped off the bed and stretched.

"I've got to move these bones."

"Are you ready for the picnic?" she asked.

He was sort of pacing around the room, picking up a book, putting it down.

"Oh yeah, sure," he said. "That'll be great. But you know, Banana, what I'd really like?"

No, she didn't.

Papa jammed his hands in his pockets and rocked on his heels.

"I'd like to blow this town. The winters here are just too dreary, and there's not enough money in it."

He was staring out her window, seeing something far away.

"What say we follow the sun and the tourists. I've always wanted to see Greece. Haven't you?"

This was the Stephen that Paula told her about, someone flying off to escape his troubles.

"No," she said.

"Think about it, Banana. It will be fun. You'll love Greece."

He was serious. It was just like when he took her away from the apple camp in France. Then she was too little to understand.

"I won't love it," she said. "I don't want to go."

"Anna!" he said. "What's the matter with you? I bet this is Paula Simmons's doing."

"No, it isn't," said Anna. *"I* don't want to leave school or my friends."

"I thought Paula was my friend," said Papa.

"She was—she is. The only thing she said was that you shouldn't have left Willow Springs."

"I told you, I had to leave. And it turned out to be the best thing I ever did, for me *and* for you."

No, it wasn't. Not for her.

"Anna, we've seen the world, at least a part of it. And there's so much more. Greece will be another chapter of our great adventure."

Another boardinghouse, another school, a *new* language. It couldn't happen. Somehow, she'd have to make him stay.

"Don't you see?" asked Papa. "Anna, I don't like you acting this way."

"And *I* don't like . . ." What could she tell him? There were too many things she hated; it was too much. ". . . this," she said, her arms flung wide open. "This!"

Papa looked at her blankly, then burst out laughing.

She slammed out of the room, past Signor Tomaso, down to Maria's kitchen.

The Signora was in the kitchen, screaming at Maria. Anna opened the door anyway and went in. The Signora whirled around.

"Now what do you want, American brat! Get out of my kitchen and stop pestering my cook."

Up close, the Signora's face was a road map of wrinkles and warts. She smelled as old and sour as the streets of Rome.

"Get out, get out, get out!"

Maria was signaling to Anna to keep silent and leave. She picked up the parcel Maria pointed to and backed out of the room.

"And stay out!" yelled the Signora. *"Brutta cattiva!* Unnatural child!"

Anna ran away from the kitchen and the Signora's curses to the dark, cluttered front hallway. She stood, trembling with anger, hemmed in by the musty furniture. She wouldn't go back to Papa, she couldn't go to Maria, and she wasn't going to stay in this dusty old hall forever. She hugged the bag and tried to think.

What an idiot she was!

That very minute, Fiorella was probably pacing up and down, waiting for her to show up. She threw open the door and raced out into the blazing sunshine.

Church bells pealed. Perhaps she was already late. She walked faster.

Bong, bong!

Most likely Paula was halfway to the airport.

Before she left, she'd written down the address for Pensione Auriga in a special book. Would she remember to send the photographs of Florry when she got back to America? Would Anna still be at the *pensione* when they came? It could be like those letters her grandmother sent. The envelope would sit forever on the mail tray under the staircase at the Pensione Auriga, turning brittle and yellow until the day Signora Rossi scooped it into the trash, throwing away the only chance she'd ever have to know what her mother looked like.

Bong! BONG!

Anna began running.

Paula had said, "He's gotten so used to running away, that's all he can do."

She hated her saying that about Papa. But it was true. He didn't want to go to Greece so they'd have more money, or for the adventure. Paula Simmons and Willow Springs had caught up with him, and he had to run away again.

Sure enough, Fiorella was waiting for her downstairs at the front entry. She rushed forward when she spotted Anna.

"*Ciao,* Anna! You're late! Where's your father?" Fiorella danced around her. "Is he sick? I like your sweater. We're still going on the picnic, aren't we?"

Finally, Fiorella stood still and looked into Anna's face.

"Anna, what's wrong?"

"Everything," said Anna. "Every single thing. Could we go on the picnic by ourselves, without my father?"

"Sure," said Fiorella. "But don't tell Babo we're going alone."

"I don't want to lie to your father."

"Don't worry," said Fiorella. "You wait here; I'll be right back."

Fiorella disappeared up the dark staircase and was back in a flash, carrying a bulging string bag.

"What did you tell him?" asked Anna.

"I said you were here, and I kissed him good-bye," said Fiorella. "Where shall we go?"

Anna shook her head. Why was it so easy for Fiorella? "Let's go to the Forum," she said. "I'll tell you about the vestal virgins."

Fiorella giggled. For the very first time that day, Anna felt all right. She could breathe. Paula. Papa. Florry. Greece. Maria. Signora Rossi. Her worries were slipping off her shoulders—not for good; they'd be back later. But now it was time out. She linked arms with Fiorella and went forward to their picnic in the remains of ancient Rome.

XII

THE ROMAN FORUM

They found some relief from the sun in the scant shade of an ilex at the edge of the parched field. All around them were broken pieces of marble and columns holding up the sky.

"So this is the Forum," said Fiorella.

"Haven't you ever been here?" asked Anna.

"Just once when I was real little."

"But you're a Roman!"

"Exactly, the Forum is for tourists and Americans."

They unpacked their bags on the cloth Anna spread on the ground. Dry grass and weeds grew up between the ancient paving stones surrounding them. Squinting tourists passed by, holding guidebooks, poring over the ruins. It was hot and quiet but for the drone of cicadas and the murmur of tourists.

"We're having veal with tuna fish," said Anna. "I hope it isn't too weird."

Fiorella looked suspicious. She sniffed the dish Anna held and took a small bite.

"Did you make this?" she asked.

"I helped Maria."

Fiorella squinched her eyes into near slits.

"Who is Maria?"

"She's the nicest person at the *pensione*. She does all the hard work for the Signora."

"Are you sure you're not really a rich *Americana?*"

"Fiorella! How can you ask that?"

"Only a rich Meez Amereeka with a fancy cook could serve *vitello tonnato* this good."

"I wish!" said Anna. "So it's edible?"

"If you don't want yours," said Fiorella, "I can eat it for you."

"Okay, okay," said Anna, taking a forkful.

Her head said weird, but her mouth said yum! She took another bite and stopped mid-swallow. This was Papa's lunch, too. The veal lodged in her throat. The Signora would never let him near the dinner table, especially considering the foul mood she was in.

"Are you all right?" asked Fiorella. "You look sort of green."

Anna swallowed hard.

"Remember, before, when I said everything was wrong."

"Yes."

"It still is."

"So, tell me," said Fiorella.

"My father wants to take me to Greece."

"You *are* rich!"

"Fiorella, this is serious. We'd go there to live and work, the same way we do here. But it would be much, much worse."

"He'd really do that?"

The look on his face this morning, she'd seen it before. It meant travel. She nodded.

"Why?" asked Fiorella. "Why does he want to take you away?"

"It's like he's running away," said Anna. "Last night we saw someone from America, someone who knew him and my mother." She was sounding like Paula. But Paula could have gotten it all wrong.

"Anna, what is it?"

"I don't know how to explain," she said. "It gets kind of confusing."

"Start at the beginning," said Fiorella.

"When my mother died, my father left America because my grandparents were going to take me away from him."

"Could they do that?"

"I don't know," said Anna. "Last night, Paula said that they really wouldn't have, that

Papa ran away because he felt bad about my mother's death and didn't want to think about it."

"What does this have to do with him taking you to Greece?"

"Maybe he wants to run away again because Paula showed up and reminded him of all the things he's been trying to forget. It's like the town he first ran away from followed him here to Rome and now he's got to run away all over again."

Fiorella looked as confused as Anna felt.

"But maybe he really is afraid my grandparents will find out from Paula where I am and come and take me away."

"I don't think I understand all this," said Fiorella.

"Neither do I," said Anna. "Paula told me that Papa should bring me back to America. If he won't, I should go there on my own."

"Wow! America! You should go," said Fiorella. "You could see Disneyland and cowboys. You could eat hot dogs."

Anna laughed. "I don't think there are cowboys in Willow Springs. Paula said I should come for Thanksgiving."

"What's that?" asked Fiorella.

"An American holiday when families get together to eat special foods and be thankful."

"For what?"

Anna shrugged. "For just being together."

For a few moments they ate in silence.

"I didn't even know you had a mother," said Fiorella.

Anna laughed. Until last night she wasn't sure she did, either.

"You have a strange sense of humor," said Fiorella.

"Well, what did you think—that I was hatched?"

"Something like that," said Fiorella.

"I *had* a mother," said Anna. "I just found out about her this morning. Paula said she was beautiful and brave."

"Like you," said Fiorella.

"Don't be an idiot," said Anna.

They finished off the veal and the spicy flat bread Maria called *foccacia*. Fiorella and her mother had made a cheesecake and a fruit salad. The food was good. It was nice eating outside with Fiorella, much better than the Signora's icy dining room. Maria would find something for Papa to eat. If he had to, there was enough money for him to go to a restaurant.

She was glad Fiorella wasn't bombarding her

with questions about her mother and Papa. For now she wanted to keep Paula's stories to herself.

"Anna, Anna! Are you here?" Fiorella asked.

"Sorry. So much has happened this morning." Anna looked at her friend. "What am I going to do?"

"What can you do?"

"There must be something. I am *not* going to Greece. They don't even have the same alphabet. If I went to school, they'd stick me in kindergarten!"

"Tell me about the Forum," said Fiorella.

"What?"

"My father says if you're stuck on one problem, move on to something else."

It was amazing how Fiorella's nutty logic made sense.

"All right," said Anna, looking around. "I'll begin here."

"Why don't you stand up," said Fiorella. "Then I can pretend you're a tour guide."

"Then I have to pretend you're an American tourist."

"Hokay-dokay," said Fiorella.

"Okey-dokey," said Anna.

She stood up, cleared her throat, and flung

The Roman Forum

out one arm, just like Papa imitating a ring-master.

"This," she said, "this is the Forum!"

"Oh yeah," said Fiorella, pretending to chew gum.

"What you see here is what's left of one of the world's greatest cities. It began with just a few huts of mud and thatch around a market-place, where the Romans and Sabines traded goods."

"Is this before or after Romulus and Remus?"

"Fiorella!"

"Just kidding," she said.

But considering Fiorella's sense of history, Anna wasn't so sure. "After," she said. *"Long* after."

"Oh," said Fiorella, smiling angelically. And Anna continued.

"This square became the center of the Republic, the glory of Rome. Citizens came here to worship their gods, honor their heroes, and elect their officials. As Rome grew mightier, marble halls were built. Columns, statues, and fountains sprung up everywhere."

"Like weeds," said Fiorella, looking at the marble ruins choked by goldenrod and chicory.

"Not exactly," said Anna. "But it got so crowded with fancy buildings there wasn't enough room left for the people to hold their meetings."

This was the story Papa told the first time he had brought her here.

"So?" said Fiorella. "What happened?"

"That was the beginning of the end. When Julius Caesar moved the Senate to another part of Rome, the power shifted from the people to the Caesars. And the Forum became a place for fortune-telling and idle gossip."

Papa had said "idle gossip" with a look of disgust. After her morning with Paula, she began to understand that look.

"How do you know all this?" asked Fiorella.

"I'm just giving you one of Papa's fifty-cent tours. I wish you could hear him. He tells it so much better. I know I'm leaving out lots of stuff."

"How does he know so much?"

Anna shrugged. Papa never seemed to *do* anything. But he was always reading something.

"He's smart," said Fiorella.

"He's too smart to be begging."

"He should be doing something else, like teaching," said Fiorella.

"He should be *working!*" said Anna. "Isn't that what all fathers are supposed to do?"

Fiorella's face got all tight and pinched looking.

"My father isn't working now, either," she said.

"I'm sorry," said Anna. "I didn't mean . . . I . . ."

"Mama says soon he'll find a good job, and I shouldn't worry."

"Please don't worry," said Anna.

"He looks in the newspaper, sends out all these letters, and goes out on interviews, but he still hasn't found a job."

"Is that how it's done?"

"How what's done?"

"Is that how people get jobs?" Anna felt a sudden inspiration; a plan began to take shape.

"Yes," said Fiorella. "I think that's about it—ads, letters, phone calls, interviews."

"Fiorella, will you help me?"

"Yes, of course."

"Let's get *my* father a job!"

"How?"

"We'll look in the newspaper, then write letters. . . ."

"What about the interviews?" asked Fiorella with a sly smile.

Anna groaned. They couldn't very well go on interviews for Papa, although it was a funny idea.

"I don't know," she said. "I'll figure that out later. First, we'll write the letters. Will your father help us?"

"Sure," said Fiorella.

"Could we tell him it's a project for school?" Anna started poking around in the dirt with her shoe, avoiding Fiorella's eyes.

"Don't worry," said Fiorella. "I am also good at keeping secrets. Yours will be safe with me."

Her own words were coming back to her. She looked up at her friend and smiled.

"Is there any cheesecake left?" Anna asked. "I'm starving!"

XIII

SCHEMING

"It's really very easy." Signor Mazzini was sitting in the crowded dining room at his makeshift desk. Newspapers, books, magazines, and ruled yellow paper covered the table and spilled onto the floor. Anna and Fiorella were perched on kitchen chairs to one side. Fiorella was taking notes.

"You begin with the proper heading, '*Egregio Signore*,'" he said, leaning over Fiorella's notepad to make sure she had the spelling right.

"What if he isn't distinguished?" asked Fiorella.

"Listen, my favorite daughter," said Signor Mazzini, "if you're going to be a pain . . ."

"All right, all right," said Fiorella. "I'll keep quiet. And, in case you forgot, I'm your *only* daughter."

"Well, that explains it," said Signor Mazzini.

"After the *proper* heading, you tell the person why you are particularly suited for this job. Don't go overboard. It's best to keep it simple."

"Could you give us an example?" asked Anna.

"For instance, Fiorella could say that her incessant, smart-aleck chatter would make her an excellent candidate for the permanent position of pain-in-the-neck daughter."

"Not funny," said Fiorella.

"But true," said Signor Mazzini. "Then you enclose a copy of your résumé, say a prayer, and send it off."

"Right," said Fiorella. "But what's a résumé?"

"Aye, Madonna. I thought you said you'd had a lesson in this? Don't they teach you anything in schools these days?"

Signor Mazzini went over it all step by step, pulling out a copy of his own résumé to explain. It told where he went to school and what he had studied. It gave a list of all the jobs he had had and when, so that every year was accounted for. That part sounded pretty important. Fiorella was furiously taking notes.

As far as Anna knew, the only job Papa had ever had was after school at the hardware store.

That wasn't something that would impress anyone.

"That's it?" asked Fiorella.

"That should do it," said Signor Mazzini. "Now can I get back to my own work?"

In Fiorella's room, they barricaded the door with one of the beds to keep out Carlo and Salvatore, then sat on the bed, reading Fiorella's notes and Signor Mazzini's résumé.

"I don't know where Papa went to school," said Anna. "I don't even know if he *finished* high school, let alone college! He's never had a real job. No one will hire him. It is absolutely hopeless!"

"Don't give up now," said Fiorella. "It's a good plan. Maybe you will have to improvise a little bit on your father's résumé."

"A little bit!" said Anna. "I'll have to invent the whole thing!"

Fiorella had this wicked little smile.

Invent the whole thing, from beginning to end. It wasn't such a bad idea. Anna flopped back on the bed with her eyes closed. All she had to do was think of jobs Papa might have had, given what he was good at.

"Teaching!" said Anna.

"You said he speaks French," said Fiorella.

"And Italian, and of course English. I

know," said Anna. "After teaching history at a famous college, he worked at the United Nations as a translator!"

"That's great!" said Fiorella.

"Now let's think of a job for Paris," said Anna. "At least we were really there."

"I know," said Fiorella. "The United Nations sent him to Paris for a conference on something important, like . . ."

"Like Vietnam!" said Anna.

It was a little weird, but it made as much sense, if not more, than their real life.

They finished off Papa's career with a stint at the American Embassy in Rome. For education, Anna gave him degrees from the University of Kansas because Paula had gone there. They decided to look through the job ads before they typed up the résumé in case they needed to add something. They borrowed the newspapers from Signor Mazzini and, each taking one, they began.

Anna looked through page after page of jobs. She had to find something that Papa might actually be interested in.

"Manicurist," read Fiorella. "Plumber's helper."

"Honestly," said Anna. "How does your father stand this? Everything looks boring or impossible. There must be a million ads for technical engineers. Aren't engineers technical enough?"

"I don't know," said Fiorella, hunched over the paper. "There doesn't seem to be much for someone who used to own a store."

"Maybe after we find something for Papa, we can help your father."

"I don't think he'd like that," said Fiorella.

Fiorella was probably right.

"Never mind," said Anna. "Your father doesn't need our help. He'll find something good all on his own."

Anna looked at Fiorella, and they both sighed. Papa wasn't going to like this much, either. But it might work if only she could find a job that would suit him as well as playing the guitar did. She went back to scanning the paper. And then she saw it. Right there in front of her in boldface type.

"Look!" she said, handing the paper to Fiorella.

"It's perfect!"

"It's more than perfect," said Anna. "It's F.A.O.!"

She snatched the paper back from Fiorella and read it over again to herself. It said:

Coordinator: Language skills, translation essential. 5 years experience Education or related fields. Doctorate in Pol. Sci. or Lang. imperative. Send pertinent material to Box 2968.

"Do you understand it all?" asked Anna.

"No," said Fiorella. "What do you suppose a coordinator does?"

Anna shrugged. All that really mattered was that it was a job at F.A.O. If she could get Papa to work there, she'd be safe. No Greece. No more begging. *And* every single lie she'd told about his working would become instantly true.

"Let's ask Babo what kind of a job it would be," said Fiorella.

"Won't he figure out we're trying to get my father a job?"

"Don't be silly," said Fiorella. "Your father already works at F.A.O. Doesn't he?"

Anna bit her lip. "Well, that *is* what I said."

After they talked with Signor Mazzini, they went back to Fiorella's room to rewrite the résumé. Anna decided to have Papa get his postgraduate degree in political science and French history.

"Yes," said Fiorella. "That sounds good. Do you know how to type?"

"Of course not," said Anna. "Can't you?"

"A little," said Fiorella. "But Mama is really good at it. Shall I ask her to do it for us?"

"How little can you type?"

"Very little," said Fiorella.

"Let me think.´. . . ." Anna chewed on a hangnail. "Yes, that would be fine. We'll erase Papa's name and address and you can type that in later."

"I'll go ask her," said Fiorella.

"Tell her our grade in writing depends on it."

"Okay," said Fiorella. "You start on the letter."

Anna sharpened her pencil and began to write. *"Egregio Signore:"*

A half-hour later when Fiorella came back with the typed résumé, she hadn't gotten much further than that.

"I can't do this," she said.

"Write what my father said," said Fiorella.

"That you would make an excellent candidate for pain-in-the-neck . . ."

"Say it the *way* he did but put *your* father in it instead of me."

"That's it!" said Anna. "Thank you, thank you, thank you!"

"*Fa niente,*" said Fiorella. "That's what friends are for. Now hurry up and write it. I've got to get started on our real homework."

"It's getting late, isn't it?"

"Mama is making supper. Do you want to stay?"

"I want to," said Anna. "But I'd better go back to Papa."

He might be really mad at her for storming out that morning. But she couldn't stay at the Mazzinis' forever.

"It will be hokay-dokay," said Fiorella. "Don't worry."

"All right," said Anna. "I won't worry about my papa, if you won't worry about yours."

"Deal," said Fiorella. "Write the letter."

She wrote that Papa "would make an excellent candidate for the position of coordinator" because of his excellent language skills and his experience in education and related fields.

"What do you think?" she asked, handing it to Fiorella.

"I think it is excellent!"

"Will your mother type it?"

"She said not to bother her again 'til after supper."

"Remember to tell her to leave space for the name and address," said Anna. "Tell her that's the way Signor Amato wants it."

"All right, don't worry," said Fiorella. "Tomorrow we'll say a prayer and post it."

"How?" she asked.

"First you buy a stamp at the tobacconist's shop," said Fiorella. "Then you put it in the letter box."

"No, don't be an idiot," said Anna. "I know how to mail a letter. What I don't know is . . ." She hesitated. It would sound as stupid as not knowing how to mail a letter. "I don't know how to pray," she said.

Fiorella started to laugh but stopped when she looked at Anna.

"It's easy," she said. "It's almost as easy as mailing a letter. You talk to God and ask him to help you. Actually, it's better if you pray to one of the saints because they were once on this earth and they can understand our problems and God can get too busy with big stuff."

"There are lots of saints," said Anna. "Which one should I talk to?"

"I bet there is someone especially in charge of helping people get work." Fiorella paused, her forehead wrinkling. "I can't remember who it is."

"It doesn't matter," said Anna. "I was just wondering."

"Pray to the Virgin," said Fiorella. "She is mother to us all, *and* she has a very important place in Heaven."

"What do I say?"

"Don't think about it too much," said Fiorella. "Just talk."

"Okey-dokey," said Anna. "I'll try it tonight. Tomorrow, let's meet ten minutes early."

"I'll be there," said Fiorella, "with the letter."

Anna said good-bye to Signor and Signora Mazzini and thanked them for helping with the homework. Fiorella walked her downstairs. Halfway down the street, Anna turned around to wave one last time to her friend.

By the time Anna reached the *pensione* and dragged herself up the stairs to their room, she could barely stand up. All the tiredness in her head had seeped down into her body. She opened the door quietly, hoping Papa wouldn't be too angry with her.

"Hey, Anna-Banana, where've you been?" said Papa without looking up.

"I was with Fiorella," she said, looking

around the room. Maps and travel brochures and other papers were spread out all over the beds and the floor. Papa was staring at something that looked like a timetable and frowning.

"I think I've got it all figured out," he said, still not looking at her.

"First, we hitchhike down the coast through Naples and Salerno. Then we cross at the ankle of Italy's boot to Bari. From there we can get on a steamer to Athens. I bet I can get a job on board to pay our way, even if it's washing dishes. I don't mind. It wouldn't be for long. Pretty good, huh, Banana? I'll tell you more about it tonight while we make our rounds."

She was too stunned to say anything and too tired to stand up one more moment. Maybe later she'd figure out an answer. But right now she had to lie down. She climbed onto her bed without bothering to move anything and closed her eyes. Her lips moved silently, shaping the words of her heart, her first prayer.

XIV

ANSWERED PRAYERS

Tuesday afternoon, Maria rushed out from the kitchen, catching Anna on her way upstairs.

"There's a letter for you on the tray," she whispered. "Tell me about it after *pranzo*." Then she raced back down the hall, ducking into the kitchen before the Signora could miss her.

The mail was left on a rickety table in the alcove under the staircase. The *vecchiette* haunted the mail tray, checking on it several times a day. Anna had never bothered to look. Who would have written to her?

She picked up the thick, cream-colored envelope. Sure enough, her name was scrawled across the front. In the upper left, embossed and gilt, was the symbol for the Hotel Nazionale and its address printed in thin brown script. Just holding the envelope felt so good, she hesitated to open it.

It had to be from Paula. There couldn't be anyone else writing to her on Hotel Nazionale stationery. Could she still be in Rome? Maybe she had missed her flight. Paula might know how to keep Papa in Rome. Maybe she'd have a better idea of how to get him a job. Anna stepped into the shadows so no one could see her and opened the letter. In the dim light she read:

Dear Anna,

My plane is leaving soon—I've only a moment to scribble this. You are so lovely, so much your mother's daughter. She'd be proud. I worry that I may have frightened you with my stories and opinions. I'd hate to think I'd brought you any unhappiness.

Losing Florry and not knowing your fate has been a great sadness in my life. Now that I've found you, I won't let you slip away again. If it wouldn't have gotten me fired, I'd have stayed longer in Rome to get to know you better.

For now, we'll have to make do with letters. Write soon.

My love to you, Dear Heart,
Paula

Paula was not in Rome. She wouldn't be able to help. But Anna needed help, the kind

Angel from Ponte Sant'Angelo

of help Paula could give. She knew Papa; she'd understand what was going on with him. Anna reread the letter. "For now, we'll have to make do with letters." Anna wanted more than letters; she wanted Paula right there, telling her what to do. But if Paula was around, Papa would probably be *more* determined to leave for Greece. Anna sighed. Letters would have to do. At least she'd be connected to America, to home. She'd borrow more money from her new-coat fund and buy some stamps.

The little old ladies were padding down the stairs. *Pranzo* would be on the table soon. Anna tucked the letter in with her homework. She'd write to Paula directly after *pranzo* and before she wrestled with any fractions.

There were so many things she'd forgotten to ask Paula when they were together. And she wanted to tell her about Maria, Fiorella, and about being the only American at La Madama. Maybe she should buy some of that thin airmail paper. Her letter might run on some, and she couldn't afford more than one airmail stamp per letter.

After Tuesday, Anna began to check the mail tray as often as the *vecchiette*. But she made sure Papa didn't catch her at it. Once she was in the alcove and out of sight, she closed her eyes and whispered a prayer.

"Let there be a letter from the F.A.O. or America." And then she opened her eyes. Papa wouldn't be happy about letters from America. Who knew how he'd feel about a letter from the F.A.O.? She'd never kept so many things secret from him. Until a few weeks ago, he knew everything she did.

On Friday she closed her eyes, made her wish, and opened them to find a large manila envelope addressed to her. The envelope was heavy and written over in English with instructions and warnings: AIRMAIL! EXPRESS MAIL! DO NOT BEND! American stamps filled the upper right-hand corner. Here was America coming to her, Anna Hopkins! She slipped it between her schoolbooks and ran upstairs to the bathroom on their landing.

Once inside with the door bolted, she ripped open the envelope. There was a letter from Paula wrapped around a stack of photographs. She flipped through the photos, looking from one to the next to the next. There was a fat-faced baby; Papa, skinny and tan on a motor-cycle; more babies; a little girl in a party dress; a girl her own age. Anna stopped. Her breathing stopped. This girl was Florry, her own mother. *Florry* scrawled on the back of the snapshot confirmed it. She looked in the mirror, then at the photo, and saw herself.

"Hey, Anna-tutta-panna," said Papa, knocking on the door. "I heard you come up the stairs. You feeling okay?"

What to answer?

"Fine," she said, without making a sound. Then louder, "Fine."

"Pranzo's ready. Come on down."

"In a minute," said Anna.

"The dragon lady won't wait," said Papa.

"I'll be there."

"Hmm."

Signor Tomaso came out on the landing and started thundering at Papa, hounding him all the way down the stairs. Anna was standing very still, staring into the mirror. Paula was right. She did look like her mother. She looked again at the picture of Florry when she was Anna's age. They could have been sisters.

She knelt down to sift through the photos she'd dropped on the floor in her rush to find a picture of Florry. On the back, each one was neatly labeled and dated. There was the farmhouse. Here was another picture of Florry, older now, in a white dress printed over with rosebuds. She was real. Anna had a real mother, and she had died. Anna slumped down onto the cold stone floor and sobbed like a baby.

After a while the storm of tears let up. She groped for more photos. There were her grand-parents. They'd always been so anonymous, she'd hardly given them a thought. But there they were, with glasses and gray hair, part of her. Her family. Fiorella always talked about her *nonna,* the mother of her mother, as if she were the Fairy Godmother.

"Little One, are you all right?" It was Maria at the door, calling softly. "Anna?"

"Just a minute," said Anna. She got up, splashed her face with cold water, and opened the door.

Maria cupped Anna's face in her warm hand. "What is it?" she asked.

Anna could barely breathe, let alone speak.

Maria's eyes went from Anna to the littered floor. She knelt to look at the photographs.

"Anna, this is your family!"

Anna sank to the floor beside her.

"These came in today's mail?"

Anna nodded.

"And this is the first time you've seen pictures of them?"

Anna leaned into Maria.

"It is wonderful! But too much wonderful,

poor Little One. And you are sitting here in this cold, damp place all alone. Take them to your room and . . ."

"No!" said Anna. Papa really wouldn't want to see these.

"You can go upstairs to my room," said Maria, carefully gathering the photos. "After I've cleaned up the *pranzo,* I'll bring you some hot tea and food."

They picked up the letter and snapshots and went up two flights of stairs, through a door, and up another very narrow staircase to Maria's room. The ceiling sloped down on one side, almost cutting the tiny room in half. But there was a window looking out over the roof gardens and red tiles, letting in the sky. The walls were bare except for a crucifix hanging over the bed and Maria's Sunday hat on a hook by the door. Anna had only been here on a few special occasions.

"The Signora would not like it for you to be here," said Maria. "You lock the door. If she comes knocking, you are quiet, okay?"

"Yes."

"I'll be back soon, Piccolina. You take care."

Maria kissed her forehead and patted her hand, almost as if she were sick. In fact, Anna felt weak and shaky. She sat on Maria's bed and one by one examined the pictures of her family.

By the time Maria returned with a tray, Anna had memorized her mother's face as a baby, a child, a teenager, and her favorite picture of her mother looking so serene and happy in the flowing white dress.

"Maria, look," said Anna, handing her the photograph.

Maria set the tray on the bed, carefully wiped her hands on her apron, and took the picture from Anna. She studied it silently for some time.

"Your mother was very happy to be carrying you."

What was Maria saying?

"Your mother is pregnant in this picture and very happy."

Anna turned the photo over to see the date penciled on the back. Maria was right. How did she know these things? Anna stared at the photograph. It was the only one of them both together. In her letter, Paula said she'd get Anna's grandmothers to send more photos, but she had wanted to get these in the mail as soon as possible.

This was real life, but it was as strange as any of Papa's stories. Florry, standing so proud and beautiful, looking straight at the camera, now straight at her, was better than a dozen magic swans.

The days passed in a dreamy haze. The thing most real to her was that picture of Florry. Papa kept talking about Greece; she refused to listen. Anna showed the photos of her family to Fiorella, telling her what stories she knew about Willow Springs.

"Florry had a little sister and brother, named Ginny and Russell. They were the ones Paula and Florry played house and school with. Ginny and Russell helped make the Four-and-Twenty Hopping Toad Pie for a Father's Day present."

"Were the toads cooked?" asked Fiorella.

"No!" said Anna. "They were alive and hopping!"

In the letter Paula sent with the photos was a family tree including all the cousins that had been born since Papa and Anna left Willow Springs. Nellie's three children were Wendy, the girl Anna played with as a baby, and two boys, Sam and Richard.

"They are just like my family," said Fiorella. "The boys are even the same ages as Carlo and Salvatore."

They played a game using the snapshots, making up silly things that Anna's family might be saying to each other. It got pretty ridiculous, but the faraway people seemed to get closer and closer.

A week went by. Every day Anna checked the mail tray for more miracles from America and, with less and less hope, for a letter for Papa from the F.A.O. Sunday she went with the Mazzinis, and every other Roman family, to the Borghese Gardens. In the late afternoon, she and Fiorella combed the Help Wanted ads for another suitable job for Papa. Nothing was worth the effort of writing another letter.

Monday, after *pranzo*, Maria called Anna to the telephone. She leapt out of her chair in the smoke-filled dining room and nearly out of her skin. No one had ever telephoned her before. It must be Paula!

It wasn't.

"Anna!" Fiorella was shouting into the phone. "I had to call you right away! We just found out! Mama said I could. It's such good news! MY FATHER GOT A JOB!"

"Oh, Fiorella!"

"It's one of those boring-sounding jobs," said Fiorella. "But he said it would be a good job *and* very secure."

"That's great!" said Anna.

"Mama is so happy, she can't stop crying. I've got to go."

It was great for the Mazzinis. They deserved some good luck. If only it were her news, too.

After school on Tuesday, Anna checked the empty mail tray before heading upstairs to drop her books and take off her jacket.

Papa flung the letter at her as she walked through the door.

"What the hell is this!"

He was so angry, everything about him looked hard and sharp.

"Read it," he said. "Read it!"

It was from the F.A.O.!

Egregio Dr. Hopkins:

We are most impressed with your credentials and background. Please call to arrange for an appointment at your earliest convenience.

It was signed by someone in personnel, followed by an address and phone number.

"What did you do for me to deserve this?" said Papa, pulling the letter away and tearing it in pieces.

It could have been a joke, but of course it wasn't, not the way he was glaring at her now.

This was exactly the letter she'd been hoping for, praying for each night. Here it was, and she didn't have the faintest idea of what to do or say. She never, ever dreamed Papa would be *this* mad. She imagined she'd say something brilliant to Papa, something to convince him how much he'd like working for the F.A.O. After all, he'd be doing something smart for a change. But there she stood, absolutely dumbstruck, not even *one* brilliant word in her head.

"Anna! What did you do?"

"I . . . I . . . I sent them your résumé." Her teeth were beginning to chatter. "They advertised in the paper and I thought—"

"That I'd like to go sit in some stuffy office and push papers around!"

"Well, yes, sort of . . ."

"No!"

He'd never shouted at her before. Her knees were actually knocking against each other.

"What is going on in there!"

The Signora was banging on the door.

"Crazy *Americani. Pazzi!*"

Papa ripped open the door. "What? What do you want?"

The Signora backed away from the door, crossing herself and mumbling about the Devil. She grabbed hold of the banister and clattered down the stairs. Anna had never seen the Signora back away from anyone before.

When Papa turned back to face Anna, his body had relaxed into its usual slouch and he was smiling crookedly.

"That'll fix her," he said, his voice sounding normal.

She took a deep breath.

"Anna, there is no way I'm going to submit to the suffocation of an office."

"There are other jobs," said Anna. Finally she was able to speak. "You could teach, or work in a restaurant, or something."

"It's all part of the same misery, and I won't get caught up in it."

How could he be so stubborn? "Everyone works," she said. "It can't be all that bad."

"Anna, you don't understand."

She didn't understand. "How could it be worse than begging?"

"You're going through a stage, Anna. You just want to be like all the other kids on the block. And you want me to be like all the other fathers."

"That's not what I want. I want . . ."

"Someday you'll be grateful for the life we've lived and the world we've seen."

No, no! She would never be grateful.

XV

EXILE

Anna sat on her bed. Papa sat on his. She had nothing to say to him. He looked at his watch. He cleared his throat.

"*Pranzo* has begun," he said. "We'd better go down. Cold heavy spaghetti is even worse than hot."

She couldn't go down to that awful, silent room. She couldn't eat, not after all the things he'd said. Papa would never get a job. He would never even try. They would go to Greece and be beggars.

"Okay," he said. "Let's go."

She sat on her bed, biting the corner of her bottom lip. She was *not* going to cry.

"Anna!" His voice was harsh and low. "Now."

She got up. She couldn't stand him shouting at her.

He was right. All the boarders were at the

table, eating their pasta and potatoes. As soon as the Signora saw them walk in, she jumped up from her chair and shrieked, "Out!" She jabbed the air with her spaghetti fork and yelled, "Not one more minute will I have these *Americani* under *my* roof. Unnatural creatures! Get out!"

Maria came up behind Anna, enfolding her in her arms. All the boarders were frozen in their seats. No one said a word. The students stared at Papa. The old ladies stared at their plates, trembling like dry leaves.

"What the Devil do you mean by that?" asked Papa.

"The Devil! *He* speaks to me about the Devil! I'm calling the *carabinieri!* Pack your bags and go!"

"All right," said Papa. "Call the police! We're leaving! After you pay back our advance."

"I owe you nothing!" The Signora was swollen and nearly purple with rage. "You and your little tramp have stolen enough food from me. The advance will be a small compensation."

"Ahem." Signor Rossi slowly stood and spoke, his voice brittle and dry. "I think you'd better leave now."

The one and only time he'd ever spoken, and

his cold words were worse than the Signora's screaming.

Anna broke away from Maria and ran as fast as she could up the stairs to hide. Angry shouts from the dining room echoed up the stairwell, until she was safe in her bed, with the pillow covering her head.

Time passed. She hugged her pillow. What would they do? Where could they go? Were the police on their way now, ready to arrest Papa? What was going to happen to her? She was rigid in her lumpy bed, wishing she could be someplace safe, or better yet, disappear altogether. There was a soft tapping at the door. Then Maria was sitting on the bed.

"Anna, Anna, you don't have to hide. It is all right. I'm here."

"Where is Papa?" she asked from under the pillow.

"He left when the Signora threw the wine bottle," said Maria. "It's better that he stays away from her now. She is mad enough to call the police, and that would mean trouble. Your father asked me to help you pack up the room.

"Anna, please look at me."

Anna released her grip on the pillow and let Maria take it away.

"It is not as awful as it seems," said Maria.

"This is a terrible place for you. I'm sure your papa will find something much better."

"He wants to go to Greece," said Anna. "That will only be worse."

"*Coraggio,* my Little One. God above will protect you." Maria hugged Anna and gently rocked her. "I will help you pack. Then, perhaps it is best that you go to your friend's home. It is not good for you to stay here."

Courage! That was the last thing she had, but she got up from the bed anyway. Maria took down their suitcases from the top of the armoire. Anna began to empty her chest of drawers and the armoire.

This couldn't be happening. It *was* happening. All her things were spread out on the bed, undies and socks too gray and thin to be out in the open. Maria folded everything into neat bundles and filled a suitcase. Her bed, her dresser, her window—none of it was hers anymore. Anna picked up her schoolbag and hugged it. The letters and pictures from Paula were safe inside. She had kept them close so that she could look at them often. Sometimes in class it was enough to touch the deckle edging of the old photographs to feel comforted. Maria stood up. Anna's possessions were all packed. Anna went to Papa's small chest to get out his things.

In the top drawer, under the worn socks, was a pile of papers. She pulled them out to place in the bottom of Papa's suitcase. The top paper was her health certificate for school, covered with official stamps and signatures. Would she be seeing La Madama again? She fanned the papers.

A tissue-thin envelope with a big red-white-and-blue American stamp caught her eye. She took it out of the pile. It was from Willow Springs, Missouri, and had arrived in Rome twelve days ago. The return address said Hopkins. It must be from her grandparents. Papa wouldn't like her going through his mail. But she had to know what it said. She took out the letter and read:

My Dear Boy,

Paula Simmons called us the minute she got back from Europe to tell us she'd found you. Your father and I are so relieved to know you and Ann are well. But we are distressed to think of the both of you living so hand-to-mouth. Think, Stephen, maybe this life of wandering is all right for you, but it cannot be good for a child. Paula said Ann seemed healthy enough, but saddled with too many worries and burdens for a young girl.

Ann deserves the best that we can *all* give her. Your father and I and Florry's parents are aching to hold that child in our arms and provide her with a comfortable, stable home. We'll send you back to college. We'll get a separate apartment for you and Ann, if that's what you want. We will do anything and everything we can to entice you back here.

Not for a moment do we doubt your love and concern for Ann. We know how precious she is to you, and by your lights, you are probably doing what you think is best. We were wrong to try to take her away from you. At that time we were so upset by Florry's death, we didn't think through what we were doing. All we saw was our boy suddenly faced with the sad burden of raising a child alone. We wanted to help. We *still* do.

We beg you to give more thought to Ann's needs. Listen to your heart, Stephen, and please, please bring that child home to us.

Enclosed is a bank check to cover the airplane tickets. Use it soon. We miss you so very much.

Your loving,
Mother

Anna stared at the check in her hand. Blood was pounding in her ears. Papa hadn't told her. *He hadn't told her!* This letter was as much hers as his. It was about her home, the home she'd been praying for. And he'd had no intention of telling her about it.

"Anna, I don't want to hurry you, but we must get you packed and out of here."

"Listen," said Anna. She translated her grandmother's letter for Maria.

"Aye, Little One," said Maria. "This is a gift from God."

Anna handed her the check.

"So many dollars! This must be millions and millions of lira!"

Every day they scrounged for fifty-lira coins. How could Papa keep this from her? He'd always been there, watching out for her, taking care of her. Now it felt like he'd pulled away and left her on her own.

"Oh, Piccolina!" said Maria, giving her a big hug. "I'm so happy for you. This will solve all your problems."

"No," said Anna. "It won't. We're not going to America. Papa wasn't going to tell me about this."

"But of course he was," said Maria.

"No," said Anna. "He's had the letter for

nearly two weeks. But all he's talked about is what fun we'll have in Greece. *That's* where he is going."

"Perhaps he was waiting to tell you later. He was keeping it for a surprise."

"No," said Anna. "The only surprise is that he didn't rip the letter to pieces the way he destroyed the letter from the F.A.O."

"My poor lamb," said Maria. "Please don't cry. Your father loves you. Perhaps this is a misunderstanding."

"Is she gone?"

It was the Signora shouting up the stair-well.

"Finish packing," said Maria. "I'll be back in a minute."

Maria left the room and stood on the stair-case, arguing with the Signora. Anna put the letter and check in her schoolbag. Then she emptied Papa's drawers, stuffing everything into his suitcase. There wasn't much left, just some books, magazines, and Papa's guitar.

The argument on the stairs got louder. There was the sound of a slap, then footsteps.

"I'm calling the police! I'm calling the *carabinieri!*"

The Signora's threats were like distant thunder. Anna was too numb to be frightened.

Maria came into the room, the left side of her face flaming.

"Are you ready?" she asked.

"Almost," said Anna. "Are you all right?"

"Yes," said Maria, her eyes blazing. "Let's go."

They put Papa's books and magazines into Anna's schoolbag. Anna carried that and Papa's guitar. Maria took the two suitcases and led the way out. Anna took a quick look around at the stained wallpaper, the cracked ceiling, and the Signora's ugly furniture before she slammed the door behind her.

Signor Tomaso came out on the landing and for once was silent. He patted Anna's shoulder, his eyes globes of sadness. As they bumped their way down the stairs and along the corridors, the *vecchiette* cracked open their doors, whispering *"Addio!"* and "Good luck!"

The street was a relief. Anna took a deep breath and looked around. It was a normal, busy, everyday sort of day. The sun was even shining. Anna's life had broken into pieces, but the rest of the world was humming along, unchanged, unaffected.

They walked down Via dei Cornacchie, the last time that street would belong to her. She was finally saying good-bye to Blackbird Street, but not as she once dreamed it would be. There was no bluebird of happiness waiting for her. There was only more care and woe.

It wasn't far to Fiorella's house, but already the straps of her schoolbag were digging into her shoulder. She needed both hands to carry the guitar so it wouldn't drag on the ground. She cradled the big, awkward case like a baby. Maria, too, was having trouble with the suitcases. She and Papa had little enough, but it was too much for Maria and her to be dragging through the streets. Papa should have been there. *He* should have carried the heavy bags. Anna hugged his guitar and went on.

The old woman who watched the entrance, the *portiera,* stopped them at the door of Fiorella's building.

"What's going on here?" she asked, eyeing them suspiciously. "Where do you think you're going?"

"The little girl is paying a visit to her friend, Signorina Mazzini," said Maria. "Surely you have seen her here many times before."

"Not with suitcases," said the old woman.

"That," said Maria, "is none of your business. Come, Anna."

Muttering about interfering witches, Maria brushed past the *portiera*.

How would the Mazzinis feel, seeing her arrive with suitcases? They were packed in pretty tight as it was.

Signora Mazzini answered the door, smiling warmly as always.

"Anna, so nice to see you. And you've brought a friend. Come in, come in."

The two women smiled at each other awkwardly. It was up to Anna to make the introductions.

"Signora Mazzini, this is my friend, Maria... Maria..." She didn't know her last name. How was it possible to know a person so well and *not* know her name?

Maria stepped forward, extending her hand to Signora Mazzini. "Maria Sartorelli," she said. "Pleased to meet you."

"And I am most pleased to meet you," said Signora Mazzini. "I've heard so much about you."

"And I, you," said Maria, putting her arm around Anna, bringing her one step closer. "I've brought Anna to you because she is in great difficulties. She's been thrown out of the house."

"How dreadful! What happened?"

"The woman who runs the *pensione* has set both Anna and her father on the street," said

Maria. "I don't think he has enough money to engage new rooms for them right now. Though I'm sure in a few days he will be able to manage it."

Fiorella came into the hall.

"Ciao, Anna. What's doing?"

Anna wished she could hide in Maria's skirts the way little children do. She glanced at Fiorella, mumbling *"Ciao."*

"Anna is welcome to stay here for as long as she wants," said Signora Mazzini.

"You are very kind," said Maria. "I know her father will be relieved. Anna, I must get back or the Signora will throw me out, too."

"Where will Papa go?"

"Don't worry, Little One," said Maria. "Perhaps my friend's cousin can find him a room. I'll tell him you are here."

Maria gave Anna a big hug and whispered in her ear. "There is no bad that doesn't bring some good with it. You'll see."

Maria slipped out the door, and Anna was left alone. The distance between her and the rest of the world seemed immense. Fiorella and her mother came forward quickly to comfort her. There was just that one long moment of terrible loneliness.

"You're staying here. Anna, I'm so glad!" Fiorella danced around her.

"Maria is right," said Signora Mazzini. "You mustn't worry now. You are safe here." She took Anna's hand.

"Gracious, child, you are so cold. And you're pale, too. Fiorella, you help Anna get settled in your room. I'll bring some soup."

Fiorella took the schoolbag, and Anna picked up her suitcase.

"These are my father's," she said, pointing to his guitar and suitcase. "Where should I put them?"

"I'll put them in this closet," said Signora Mazzini, "out of reach of the barbarians."

Once in Fiorella's room, they barricaded the door.

"Tell me what happened," said Fiorella.

It seemed as if ten awful things had happened all at once. Right now, Anna was too tired to tell it all.

"The Signora kicked us out," she said. "And this is what I found when I was packing Papa's things." Anna dug into her bag and pulled out the letter and check.

"What is it?"

"A letter from my grandmother, telling

Papa to bring me home, to America. And there's a check for the plane tickets."

"That's incredible! Fabulous! It's hokay-dokay! Oh, no! It means you're leaving."

"I *may* be leaving," said Anna. "But not for America. I'll never see it. Papa will be taking me to Greece."

"You could go alone," said Fiorella.

"What? Where?"

"To visit your grandparents," said Fiorella. "Last year I went by myself to Sicily to see my father's parents."

Anna couldn't go to America without Papa.

"It was great," said Fiorella. "The airline people were really nice. They kept bringing me sodas and snacks. They even gave me a backpack filled with games."

It didn't matter how nice the airline people were.

"I don't want to go by myself," said Anna.

"It wasn't scary," said Fiorella.

But it *would* be scary. Anna had never been anywhere without Papa. She couldn't even imagine it.

"I couldn't do it," said Anna.

"Why not?" said Fiorella.

"Because." Because she couldn't. It was absolutely impossible.

XVI

LIMBO

The phone rang just as Anna and the Mazzinis sat down to supper. The boys jumped up from their seats as if it were the starting gun for a race.

"Carlo! Salvatore! Sit down!" said Signor Mazzini. "I'll get it."

He answered the phone in the hall.

"Ah, Signor Hopakinza!"

Papa! Was he safe? Had he found a place to sleep? She wanted to know but dreaded talking to him.

"No, no, no trouble at all. We're delighted to have her."

Signor Mazzini made it sound as if Anna were there for a pajama party. Both of Fiorella's parents acted as if her being there were perfectly natural. And neither of them seemed shocked that she and Papa had been living in a *pensione*.

Maybe they never believed Fiorella's stories of the Palazzo Americano.

"Anna," said Signor Mazzini, coming back to the table, "it's your father."

"Thank you," said Anna. She went to the hall and picked up the receiver. She stood staring at the coil of black phone cord, trying to see the Papa she'd always believed in, the one she'd always loved.

"Hi," she said.

"Hey, Anna-Banana! You okay? Hope that old witch didn't scare you too much."

"No," said Anna.

"Well, let's take the night off, anyway. We've had enough excitement for one day."

"I'm not singing anymore," said Anna, barely above a whisper.

"What, Banana?"

Did she really say that? Yes. She did.

"I don't want to sing with you anymore," said Anna, loud and clear into the phone.

"All right, Annalina. I don't want you to do anything you feel strongly against."

He sounded hurt.

"Papa, I mean singing at the restaurants."

"Yes, Anna. I understand. It's all right. Don't fret yourself inside out. We'll talk more tomorrow after your school."

Fountain of the Turtles
Piazza Mattei

"Did Maria find you a room?"

"Yes, Annalina. I'm snug as a bug. See you tomorrow. I'll come round to fetch you."

"Okay," said Anna.

"Anna," said Papa. "Anna . . . don't worry, okay?"

"Okay."

There was a click and then the buzz of the dial tone, which she listened to for some moments before laying the receiver back in its cradle.

She went back to her seat at the table. In front of her was a plate piled high with pasta and beans. Anna pushed a bean around with her fork. How could he be so kind and still refuse to understand that what she needed was something as normal and solid as a plate of spaghetti and beans in a home of their own?

"Anna," said Signora Mazzini. "You look so tired. Would you like to be excused?"

She nodded. It was true. She was too tired to eat or even to sit. She got up from the table.

"I'm sorry," she said.

"For what?" asked Signora Mazzini. "Lie down. Feel better. I'll bring you some warm milk."

"Can I lie down, too?" asked Salvatore.

"Pazzino!" said Signor Mazzini. "Noodle-head, sit down and eat your supper."

Anna walked down the dark hallway to the room she was sharing with Fiorella and her brothers. She took off her shoes and climbed onto the cot she and Fiorella had made up earlier. It was jammed in between the beds and up against Fiorella's nightstand. The foot of the cot nearly touched the dresser opposite. All afternoon the boys practiced squeezing through, hopping over, and crawling under the cot to get to their beds. That was, until Signor Mazzini got home from his new job and put a stop to it.

Anna lay on her back, the covers pulled up around her chin. Watching Carlo and Salvatore was the one happy moment of the day. She rolled over to her side. She could feel the wrinkles being pressed into her school clothes. They'd be a mess by the morning. She really should get up and put on her nightgown. But that was too much for now.

"Anna, are you awake?" Fiorella called softly from the door.

"Yes," said Anna, her eyes still closed. "I'm awake."

"I've brought your milk."

"That's nice," said Anna. She should open her eyes, but the lids were too heavy.

"Anna, are you sick?" Fiorella was on her bed next to Anna.

"I don't think so. I'm tired."

"Can you drink this?"

Anna opened one eye.

"Should I?"

"Yes."

She pulled herself up on an elbow and took the warm glass. Signora Mazzini had sprinkled cinnamon on the frothy milk.

"I have to go help with the dishes," said Fiorella. "I'll see you later."

"Thanks for the milk," said Anna.

When Fiorella left the room, Anna drained the glass and slumped down under the covers. Maybe she *was* sick. Her head was so heavy. Her arms and legs were leaden. If she was sick, she could just stay in this bed and drink warm milk. Papa couldn't take her to Greece if she were sick. If she was really sick, wouldn't he have to take care of her? Wouldn't he *have* to get a job and make everything all right?

No. No! That was a little kid's dream. He was not going to get a job. He was not going to get them a real home. He was not taking her to America.

He wasn't going to suddenly become someone different from whom he was just because she wished it so. And would she want him to be all that different? What she really wanted to change was her own life.

"Great change requires great courage." Maria had said that.

Anna groaned and rolled over to her other side. That afternoon Fiorella had made her trip to Sicily to see her grandparents sound so easy. But no matter what Fiorella had said, the idea of a long journey alone was terrifying. Anna turned from one side to the other, trying not to think. And finally sleep came.

She dreamed she was on an airplane surrounded by sunny stewardesses offering her sweets and games, pillows and blankets. But something was very wrong with the picture. The seat next to her was empty and Anna was crying. One of the stewardesses became Maria. She put her arm around Anna and whispered in her ear, *"Coraggio!"*

Anna awoke during the night, staring into the blackness, her heart racing. Where was she? The heavy breathing of Fiorella and her brothers anchored her and soon sent her back into a deep sleep.

When she awoke again the room was sunlit and Signora Mazzini was sitting on Fiorella's bed holding a cup of hot chocolate. The other beds were empty.

"They've been gone for hours," said Signora Mazzini. "Somehow you slept through this morning's chaos."

"What about school?"

"Today you needed sleep. I wrote a note to your teacher, and Fiorella will help you with the assignments tonight."

Anna felt as if she'd survived a shipwreck. She sat up and took the hot chocolate.

"Did Fiorella tell you what happened?"

"Yes, she explained," said Signora Mazzini. "She also told me about your grandmother's letter."

"What should I do?"

"Have breakfast," said Signora Mazzini. "And then you must talk this over with your father."

That seemed simple enough, so why was it so dreadful?

Anna spent the next few hours waiting for Papa and thinking the unthinkable. Could she go by herself to America? Yesterday Fiorella had made it sound so easy. Nothing was that easy. Going to America meant losing Fiorella as well as Papa.

Going to America. It could also mean going home to the kind of home she'd been praying for, to a place where she belonged. America could be what she'd always wanted, or it could be like starting in a new school—only a thousand times worse. What if there wasn't a Fiorella in Willow Springs? What if the kids were all like Gina and Teresa? Her grandmother had said they wanted her. But her grandmother didn't even know her. What if her grandmother turned out to be like Signora Rossi? Anna read her grandmother's letter again and again.

No. Her grandmother sounded nice. Anna studied the photographs Paula sent. Both her grandmothers looked nice, much more like Signora Mazzini than Signora Rossi.

Anna took a long bath and put on the freshly ironed clothes Signora Mazzini had ready for her. She made her bed and helped prepare *pranzo.* Her eyes were open, her hands were busy, she talked with Signora Mazzini about the cooking and school and Maria. And every single minute, she was thinking about America and waiting for Papa. Everything else seemed to be happening to someone else.

Soon after the midday church bells, Signor Mazzini arrived with Carlo and Salvatore. The boys dropped their schoolbags and raced down the hall, ripping off their smocks. There was the clatter of their heavy shoes and the ping of a button hitting the marble floor.

"Aye, Madonna!" exclaimed Signora Mazzini. "Every day another button."

Some time later, Fiorella appeared, adding her satchel to the pileup in the hall.

"Ciao, Anna!"

Fiorella dragged Anna into the bathroom to talk privately.

"Signor Amato thinks you are really sick. He said not to worry about the test. You can do a makeup."

"What test?" said Anna.

"Gina said you were faking it, so I told her to 'Flayco offay!'"

"You mean, 'Flake off'?"

"Si, si, si. Flayco offay. Are you all right?" Fiorella stopped talking long enough to look at her.

"I will have to leave Rome," said Anna.

"You'll be going to America, to your grand-parents," said Fiorella.

"I doubt Papa will head in that direction."

Fiorella shrugged. "Who knows?" she said. "Anything can happen."

"We'll be too far apart to be friends," said Anna.

"Who says!" Fiorella looked furious. "Just because you go to a different country, you will stop being my friend?"

"No," said Anna. "I didn't mean I wouldn't like you anymore. It's just that it's so far."

"Aren't you going to write to me?"

"Of course, I'll write," said Anna.

"Every week?" asked Fiorella.

"Every week," said Anna. "But . . ."

"Good," said Fiorella. "I'm glad that's settled." She gave Anna a hug. "When I come visit, you will take me to Disneyland, yes?"

"Yes," said Anna. "Sure thing."

Disneyland! If Fiorella understood geography, she might be worried, too!

BLUEBIRD

Papa arrived just as Anna and Fiorella were clearing away the *pranzo* dishes. The Mazzinis tried to get him to sit down and eat something.

"At least have a *caffé?*" asked Signor Mazzini.

"No, thank you," said Papa. "It's very kind of you but . . ."

"Perhaps later?" said Signora Mazzini.

"Thank you, yes," said Papa. "Later."

He and Anna went outside to a day clear as glass. Papa led Anna along the familiar streets; he looked rumpled and vague, just as he always did. He was singing bits of all of Anna's favorite songs. His voice carried her along. She could follow him anywhere.

They entered at the north end of Piazza Navona and crossed the field of cobblestones to Café Navona. Papa stepped up to the cashier and ordered cappuccino, *caffé,* and one *cannole.*

He brought the receipt to the barman, plunking down some change in the tip dish. Anna bit into the *cannole* as soon as the barman set it in front of her.

"Will one be enough?" asked Papa.

"Mmmm," said Anna. They really couldn't even afford one, but she wasn't going to say that now.

They drank their coffee in silence. Anna had worried so much this morning about what she would say to him that not saying anything was quite a relief. When they'd finished, Papa ambled out of the café and past the fountain to plant himself on a bench in front of the church. Anna sat next to him. Now she had to speak.

"I found the letter," she whispered.

"So, what do you think?"

"I think you should have told me about it."

"I wasn't quite ready," said Papa. "I needed some time. But I am sorry you found it first."

Her anger left her like a deep sigh. She moved closer, breathing in the warm, clean smell of his old cotton shirt. Papa put his arm around her and kissed the top of her head.

"Annalina, I'm leaving for Greece as soon as I can."

"I don't want to go there." Anna said it softly, but Papa heard her.

He nodded.

"I'm sending you to my folks in Missouri. You can go to school in Willow Springs."

"No!" said Anna. "I can't go alone."

Papa turned her gently to look into her face, his gray eyes clouded.

"Are you worried about the traveling part?" he asked.

"No. Maybe," said Anna.

"I checked it out with the airline," said Papa. "They'll take good care of you."

"But how can I go there without you?"

"Anna, I think you need to go," said Papa. "You've been telling me, and I just didn't want to hear it. You need the kind of home my mom and dad can give you."

He had heard her after all.

"I can't give you that, not yet. Maybe Paula was right—I don't know. Someday I'll settle down and get a job. When that day comes, will you write my résumé?"

"Oh, Papa." Anna started to laugh, but it came out more like a sob.

"It's okay, Annalina. Everything will be all right."

Papa was holding her hand, stroking each finger. "Remember when I used to call you Monkey Paws?"

Anna nodded. That was a long time ago.

"Anna, I'm sending you to family. They'll take good care of you. Besides," he said, his face brightening in a mischievous grin, "it's not forever, Anna. I thought next summer we'd meet up somewhere."

"What! I mean, where?"

"Wherever you like," he said. "I can save up enough money for your fare. We could go apple picking in France or rendezvous in Rome. Being a summertime free spirit might appeal to you."

Rome in the summertime! She could see Maria and Fiorella. There'd be time for picnics and trips to the beach at Ostia.

"Would we still be street singers?"

"That would be up to you," said Papa.

"Would we live on Blackbird Street?"

"No," said Papa, smiling. "Never again!"

Come back to Rome? Papa had opened a door she'd never considered. Yes, she could do that. But what about America on her own? Could she do *that?*

"Will they like me in America?" she asked.

"Annalina," said Papa, hugging her tight, "you read my mom's letter. They'll eat you up."

He rocked her in his arms.

"Mom and Florry's mother will spoil you as much as they possibly can."

He held her for a while without speaking, then he laughed.

"Nellie will try to boss you. She always *tried* with me. You just 'Yes, ma'am' her, then go on about your business."

"Her daughter, Wendy, is my age," said Anna.

Papa looked hard at her.

"Yes. Wendy will be in your same class. She'll help you out at school."

"It will be different," said Anna.

"Yep," said Papa. "I think it will make a nice change from Signora Rossi's House of Horrors."

Anna laughed, then stopped. No Signora Rossi. No Maria, either.

"Will *I* like it?" she asked.

"Yes, Banana, I think you will. Give it time and don't fret. It will be different from life as you've known it. It will be different from Rome."

"Will you be all right?"